From Fame to Shame

VERONICA BLADE

PUBLISHING

Gardnerville, Nevada

From Fame to Shame

Crush Publishing, Inc.
1291 Bolivia Way
Gardnerville, NV 89460
www.CrushPublishing.com

ISBN 978-0-9853434-1-5

Cover design by Rose Nomura

Edited by Sarah Billington & Robin Haseltine

From Fame to Shame
Excerpt

"And what are your plans later tonight?" Dallas reached up to rub a lock of my hair between his thumb and finger.

"Plans?" My mouth went dry. He stood way too close and my concentration slipped.

"You always have plans." His eyes caressed my face.

"Not tonight." Somewhere deep in my soul, I knew that was the wrong answer. It opened the door to a date with him, which would lead straight to trouble. But when your brain stops working, telling the truth is so much easier.

"A friend told me that Josh Adams is jamming at Hanks Blues tonight."

I nodded, since it was all I was capable of at the moment.

"We'll have dinner there. I'll pick you up at six."

Preventing Dallas from making another date with me would've been smart. The words hovered in my throat, but I couldn't force them out. Even if I didn't reject his offer, I needed to say something. Or, at the very least, finish cleaning up after breakfast. And yet, I couldn't move. I just stared into his eyes as they fixed on mine.

His gaze fell to my mouth, then he reached both hands up to cup my face and, inch by inch, brought his mouth to mine.

Our lips touched, feather-light. He shifted his body and brought his thighs against mine, but he didn't deepen the kiss. He just skimmed the surface, gently teasing my mouth until my body hummed. Seconds stretched and my lungs stilled as I waited for his next move.

Then, slowly, he withdrew, keeping close enough that I still felt his warm breath against my skin.

I couldn't catch my breath. A thick haze clouded my brain and I worried he might ask me something, anything, that required a response and I'd slip up. Fear that I'd blow it for Jackie paralyzed me.

Oh, my God! Jackie! If she knew I'd just kissed the guy who dumped her, she'd be hurt. Jackie didn't need that, on top of everything else.

"I…" I had no idea what to say. I only knew that if someone didn't say something soon and break the trance, I would betray Jackie worse than I already had. Because, more than anything, I wanted this guy, no matter how *nice* he was.

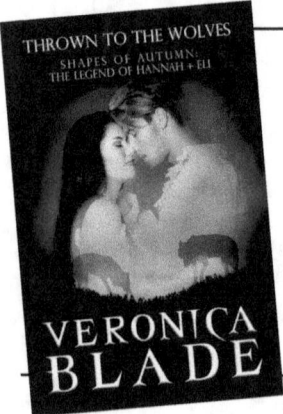

For Debra, April, Ashley & Julie—
y'all make me feel like a rock star!

Chapter One

After confirming the apartment number on the door, I inserted the key Jackie mailed me weeks ago and darted inside her condo without knocking. My twin sister jumped, jostling a glass near her hand — as if any paparazzi could sneak their way into her secure building. Her blue eyes sparked with recognition as her breath whooshed out.

"Sorry to scare you," I said. "Got going early this morning since you said it's urgent." I set my purse on the chair next to her. "Didn't you get my text a couple hours ago?"

"Yeah, I'm just jumpy." Jackie dropped the thick stack of papers — probably a screenplay from her agent — and it thumped onto the shiny glass tabletop. An instant later, she was hugging me. "I'm so glad to see you, Maddie."

The stress of the two-hour drive in LA traffic dissipated as I melted against her. My eyes scanned the spacious dining room and living room, landing on the window that stretched the length of the wall. No wonder Jackie had been so excited about her new place. The view of the hills made you forget you were in the city. The best of both worlds.

With Jackie's seven-figure paychecks, she could afford a Hollywood mansion. But she liked the idea of the doormen and security. She also didn't want to hassle with the extra staff to keep up the house and grounds.

"You owe me big time." I squeezed gently, then noticed who else was in the room. "Hi, Stella."

Jackie's loyal assistant wore a slinky black dress more suited for clubbing than working. But this was Hollywood and when you worked for someone like Jackie, you dressed the part. Stella did anyway. With her heels, she towered over me. Not that she needed any help. At five-two, most people dwarfed me. Probably why Jackie always wore those dangerous shoes that elevated her five inches.

Stella glanced from me to Jackie, then back again. "It's weird seeing you two together. If you had highlights, Maddie, and straightened your hair, I'd totally think you were Jackie."

Jackie always spent extra time on her hair and face. I'd skipped the makeup today and let my hair go naturally wavy, as usual. Well, not actually wavy. More like bent or crooked.

"Why don't you take your lunch break now?" Jackie asked, handing Stella a fifty dollar bill. "It's on me today. Give us a half hour to catch up."

"You sure? I thought you needed me to — "

"I do," Jackie said. "But it's way past lunchtime. We'll deal with that when you come back."

Stella hesitated, then opened her mouth like she wanted to object. "You're the boss." Shaking her head, she flipped her blond hair before grabbing her bag and disappearing out the door.

"I'm sorry I made you ditch school," Jackie said.

I raised my brows. "You went to my high school graduation two weeks ago. Wake up and smell my schedule, sis. College doesn't start until the fall."

"Oh, yeah, I forgot. I guess I've had too much going on." She stood near her wrought-iron chair as if rooted to the floor, her voice shaky — nothing like the confident, spunky girl who'd struck out on her own to become a Hollywood starlet.

"So, are you going to finally spill why you dragged me here?" I asked.

"You know I'd never ask you to leave Podunk for civilization unless I was desperate, right?" Jackie pressed her lips together, brows drawn.

Jackie was a lot of things — impulsive, sometimes reckless — but she wasn't manipulative. And she never relied on family to bail her out. I had thought the emancipation two years ago at age sixteen was a bad idea, and so did my parents. But Jackie had surprised us all and survived just fine. If she asked something of us, she had a damn good reason.

"That's why I'm here," I said. "You should finish gathering whatever you want to bring, so we can be out of LA before rush hour." Jackie made a big production out of packing, always paranoid she forgot something. If I didn't push her now, I'd be stuck in town another day.

"Actually...I was hoping you'd stay." She crossed her arms over her stomach, chin quivering as her eyes pooled with tears.

No way. Tears or no tears, Jackie was asking an awful lot of me, especially when all she had to do was slip into the passenger side of my car to escape whatever crisis she refused to divulge. Very little effort on her part if I did all the driving the whole way back.

I groaned. "Don't you remember what happened last time I was here?"

Jackie gave a watery laugh. "Oh, c'mon, you have to admit that was fun."

"Running from paparazzi and having to hide in a gas station bathroom, because they think I'm Jackie Bloom, is *not* my idea of a good time." I rolled my eyes, then turned and made my way to the refrigerator.

"Please, Maddie. " Her voice went tight. "I need you here."

My spine straightened as I grabbed a can of soda. When I returned to the dining room, Jackie was sitting in the chair, her hands folded in her lap. She appeared so much more vulnerable. "What's going on?" I asked.

A sob escaped her. "I'm done, Maddie. I can't take it anymore. I just need to go home."

Done with Hollywood? Not in a million years. My twin sister lived to act, craved the attention and shined in front of the camera. It fed her soul. Even if Jackie had the urge to abandon her dreams, she'd surely be more miserable away from the limelight than she was now. She just needed some time to realize how much she missed it.

"Then let's go." The top of the can hissed when I popped it. "We can be on the road in five minutes if you get a move on."

"I still have important contractual obligations here." Jackie looked up at me with huge eyes. "If I break them, I'm screwed. But if I stay here I'll crack, Maddie. You have to pretend to be me. Just for a week or so…"

I snorted, leaning a hip into the dining room table. "Yeah, right."

"Filming doesn't start on *Worlds Apart* for a few weeks and *Back in the Days* is on hiatus right now. So there's no acting involved, other than, you know, acting like me. I'm just committed to finishing the publicity for *Breathless*. If I don't do it, my reputation in Hollywood is shot. All you'd have to do is show up to a few events and smile for the camera."

Oh. My. God. She was serious.

I rarely wavered in my disdain for everything Hollyweird. What can I say? It's just not for me. Except for Jackie's sleek, black Tesla Roadster that starred in a few of my dreams as I whooshed down Pacific Coast Highway. Then there was her superstar boyfriend. He'd been my fantasy guy long before Jackie ever moved next door to him.

Guys that hot were used to getting any girl they

wanted and, to me, relationships didn't have room for super-sized egos. No, Dallas Bines was strictly fantasy, just like the car. Besides, he was dating my sister.

Being Jackie Bloom, no matter how temporary, was out of the question. Staying in Hollywood would mean suffering through traffic, inhaling bad air, and being around too many damn people. But as annoyed as I was to be this far from the security of my parents' house on the outskirts of Hemet, her quivering lip concerned me.

I softened my voice and moved to stand in front of her. "Turn it all over to your lawyer, then come home with me and drive back when you're feeling better. Problem solved."

"Maddie…" Her eyes glistened with unshed tears.

My eyes snapped to hers. "Impersonating someone else is fraud. There has to be another way."

"Every other way out involves more humiliation."

I set my soda on the table to bend down and touch her arm. "Tell me what happened."

"There was this guy." She wiped her cheeks with the tips of her fingers. "He was charming, funny and sweet. And insanely hot."

"Wait. What about Dallas?"

She tilted her head. "What about him?"

"I thought he was your boyfriend."

"Guess I forgot to tell you." She choked on a sob. "He dumped me."

"Oh, Jackie," I said. "I'm so sorry." I did my best

to avoid the celebrity gossip pages, but it felt wrong that the rest of the world knew more about Jackie's life than her own sister.

She waved it away with her hand, then lowered her gaze. "We're cool now. He's way too nice for me anyway. Still, getting dumped, even if I know it's for the best, makes for serious damage to the self esteem."

"Doesn't he live right across the hall?"

Jackie shrugged. "Yes. Guess I shouldn't date where I live, huh?"

"Hmm." I grabbed the nearest chair and sat, scooting close to her. "So this new guy's an actor or musician?"

She sniffed. "Musician. Older, like twenty-something. I should've known he was too good to be true."

"Yeah." Unfortunately, I *did* know. Not with musicians, of course. But I had my share of bad luck with guys who only wanted to date me, because they thought I looked like the famous Jackie Bloom. Now, I was extra cautious and rarely ever dated.

Jackie grimaced. "I had Pete over one night and Dallas saw us outside my door. Get this. Dallas knows him through a friend of a friend. So the guy who dumped me, Dallas, was the one who informed me that the new guy was married. How screwed up is that? Explained why Pete never wanted to be seen with me publicly. Jerk."

"Ouch." It wasn't like Jackie to let a guy drive her out of town though. "So what else?"

She took a shaky breath. "Henley White is looking to cast his next movie, *Winter's Edge*. It's about a girl who loses everything—Scarlett O'Hara meets the Great Depression. Pretty intense. We're talking, kill your own food and skin it, then use the fur to keep warm. A part like that would open the door for more serious roles."

I brushed a soggy lock of hair off her tear-stained cheek and tucked it behind her ear. "What does this movie have to do with your bad taste in guys?"

"Somehow word got out that I was interested in that role and, next thing I knew, it was this big deal and everyone had an opinion. 'Jackie Bloom is washed up.' 'Jackie's not good enough for that part.'"

"Don't listen to them, Jackie," I said. "I don't think Henley White would."

"He wants his movie to be a blockbuster. Having a star who's getting ridiculed isn't going to help him sell tickets." Jackie covered her face with her hands. "All the talk shows were making fun of me. God, Saturday Night Live even did a skit. They had me showing up to the set wasted."

That was a little extreme. Sure, Jackie sometimes drank, like a lot of teens our age did. And, yes, she had one highly publicized drunken incident where she fell in a fountain. Other than that, she didn't usually have more than one drink, especially not while she was working. Her career was too important to her.

Of course, she'd been known to date guys like rocker Jimmy Zee of The Hard Drivers who'd had a sex video leaked at the tender age of seventeen. With that in mind, her choices didn't exactly discourage criticism.

On the other hand, that tape was quite a sell. Judging by the covers of gossip rags, Jackie wasn't the only one whose interest had been piqued.

"I had no idea all that was going on." I stroked the back of her hair. "It'll blow over. Just wait it out."

"Yeah, they'll forget about it eventually." Jackie leaned over and cried into my shoulder. "But I won't. I feel lost, Maddie, like a part of me is broken. Acting is all I've ever wanted to do, but apparently the tabloids think I should do something else."

"Tabloids are part of being in the spotlight." I stroked her hair. "You're an awesome actress and you worked your butt off to land a hit TV show. Tabloids profit every time a celebrity makes a mistake. But no one's perfect and other people understand that. You just need thicker skin."

"It still hurts. Oh, Maddie, I've never wanted anything like I want that part. My agent heard Henley is considering Phoebe Owen. What if he decides on her?" Jackie said something else, but it got muffled in a sob. A couple minutes later, she lifted her head and wiped her eyes.

"Come home, sweetie. There's got to be some clause or loophole to get you out of whatever they want you to do," I said.

Jackie squeezed her eyes shut and shook her head. "There isn't. I checked. And if word gets out that I've breached a contract, I could kiss that role goodbye forever. Or any other decent role."

"Jackie, this is just…the *worst* idea ever." I stifled

the rising angst.

"Please, Maddie. Be me for a few days. I'll do anything. I'll—" She froze and gripped my wrist. "I'll give you my car."

I inhaled and choked on a gulp of soda, bubbles fizzing up my nose. I stood up as an image of me cruising in the Tesla Roadster all the way to Hemet, wind blowing through my hair, flashed through my mind. I forced myself to mentally brush it away. I loved that car, but it wasn't worth the hounding I'd endure from the paparazzi.

"It isn't just me," I said. "Mom and Dad need help at the store."

"I can be you. Besides, I had that job and I know the difference between blue topaz and sapphire. A quick refresher on inventory and bookkeeping and I'm set."

"You were fifteen and way more interested in boys. You sucked at that job." I scrunched up my nose. "Sorry."

Jackie's scheme *so* wasn't going to happen. I paced the dining room.

"Ouch." She covered her heart protectively and faked a pout. "But if Mom and Dad don't object, why should you? It's *their* store. I'll hide in the back, like you do. You'll still have your phone in case your friends call."

At least Jackie was thinking it through. Still… "No one but Mom and Dad would know?" I asked.

She gave me her *Are you crazy?* look that she did so well. "Being myself to anyone else would defeat the whole purpose of swapping places with you. Stella's the only exception, since she knows every detail of my life and you'll need her help."

I thrust a hand up, palm spread. "Have you totally lost it? I'm so sorry you're going through this, but your plan will never work. Too many things can go wrong. We just need one person to notice anything different about me — I mean you — and they'll immediately think of me."

"Why would they suspect anything? I've never told a soul, other than Stella, that I even have a twin."

She'd never told anyone? My brows furrowed and my gaze drifted to the hardwood floors. I'd been too grateful for my privacy to question why none of the magazines ever mentioned Jackie's twin. "Yeah, but secrets are harder to keep when you're in the public eye."

Her eyes pooled again and she rose to meet my gaze, then held my hands in hers. "Please, Maddie. I'm begging you."

Jackie had always been the tougher one of us, bailing me out of jams. Like the time she'd switched places with me, so I wouldn't have to speak in front of the class. Now she needed me. But could I get away with impersonating her in front of the whole world?

"What if you run into someone I know?" I asked.

"You're kidding, right?" she scoffed. When I answered her with a blank stare, she continued. "I'll fake it, of course. I pretend to be other people *for a living.*"

True. Besides, I lived with my parents in a small, retirement town — hardly the type of people who searched the internet for gossip on teen starlets. And, unlike me, Jackie piled on makeup to run a simple errand the same way she did for filming. And she always made a fashion statement. I did the exact opposite, usually in sweats or jeans and a ponytail, and easily flew under the public radar.

It might work…

I shook my head as the last little bit of my resolve slipped. Could it be that easy pretending to be Jackie? "You have highlights in your hair. I don't."

"Everyone will just assume I got tired of them. When I come back, they'll think I missed the highlights and put them in again." She gently squeezed my hands. "It'll work, Maddie."

I'd thought Jackie was insane to move to Hollywood, but when she set her mind to something, she did it. If Jackie believed I could swap places with her, maybe I could.

I stopped staring at the floor and met the desperate, but hopeful look on my twin's face. My sister. My other half.

Oh God. I was about to become Jackie Bloom.

Chapter Two

"I'm going to kill her. How did she talk me into this?" I punched the decorative pillow in my lap and brooded.

"That's what I ask myself on a daily basis." Stella chuckled.

Jackie swept back into the living room and dropped a suitcase by the door. Finally. She and Stella had spent at least two hours going over Jackie's itinerary for the next several days and briefing me on anyone I could possibly encounter. Then she'd spent over an hour gathering her stuff. The sooner she left, the sooner she could get on with her sabbatical and the sooner I'd be done with the charade.

I rose from the sofa to see her off.

"Thank you so much for doing this, Maddie. I owe you big time." She sighed. "I don't know what I'd do without you."

I scrunched up my nose. "Just don't alienate my friends back home."

"You worry too much." Jackie gave me a big hug. "Love you."

My stomach tightened. I could do this. "Love you, too."

"Oh, I almost forgot." She reached into her purse and pulled out her wallet.

"What do I need that for?"

"You need my ID if someone asks for it. You're me, remember? And if you want to buy something, your ID has to match the plastic. We'll trade."

I flinched. Handing over my ID and credit cards made it so much more real. For the next few days or weeks, I wouldn't be me. I wouldn't even have my faithful Volkswagen Beetle. I'd have her Tesla though. And Jackie needed this. I'd do it for her. In a daze, I rifled through my purse, then offered up my wallet.

"You're going to do great. Thanks again. Really." She snatched my wallet, gave me another hug and darted through the door.

Stella closed the door after Jackie, then glanced at the legal pad she'd been making notes on. "I think we covered any situation that could pop up. Other people in the building you might run into, upcoming appearances. But if you forget something, I'm familiar with most everyone she knows, so I can give you a refresher any time. If I'm not here, you can reach me on my cell. All you need to do is stick to the plan and not leave this condo without me. Okay?"

I nodded.

"I'll be back here at eight in the morning. We've

got that movie premier tomorrow night. You — I mean Jackie — had to send the dress back for alterations. They swore they'd have it ready, but just in case it's still not quite right when we get there, I'd like us to arrive early."

"But you guys already worked out the dress stuff. What problem could there be?" I asked.

"Jackie's the one who fitted for the dress. You two look the same weight, but you never know." She shrugged.

I didn't want to go gown shopping for myself, much less Jackie. I'd rather be in jeans and a tee. Besides, I'd surely end up with something Jackie Bloom wouldn't be caught dead in. "What are we going to do if it doesn't fit?"

"We'll figure it out. Believe me, I'm highly motivated to convince everyone you're Jackie. If we pull this off, Jackie's promised me a big, fat bonus." Stella grinned. "Gotta go. I have a date."

"Have fun. See you tomorrow," I said, returning her smile as she waved and left.

From the black leather sofa, I glanced around the room and willed my muscles to relax. Okay, so staying here wasn't exactly a hardship. I had all the modern luxuries — gleaming, hardwood floors, a giant kitchen, more bedrooms than I needed and the biggest TV I'd ever seen in my life. Then there was the gorgeous balcony with a dazzling view of the Hollywood Hills. I'd think of this as a vacation. All I had to do in between was make a few appearances.

Posing for the camera wasn't difficult and I could be

charming when I wanted to. In front of hundreds of people? No problem. Except my body disagreed, butterflies making war in my stomach. I seriously needed to chill.

Darting to the kitchen, I brewed some herbal tea, then made myself comfortable again on the sofa. I turned on the TV and flipped through stations.

At home in my own room, reading kept me happy, but I hadn't thought to pack a book or my e-reader since I'd only planned on a day trip. Getting lost in an epic romance novel would've made me forget, at least temporarily, that I'd only brought pajamas, one change of clothes and my camera. I could download the ebook app on my phone, I supposed, but I so preferred the bigger screen of the reader. Not having my belongings made me feel out of sync and being alone in Jackie's huge condo didn't exactly put me at ease.

I switched off the TV and rolled my shoulders. My friends often teased me for being a hermit, because I often opted for the comfort of my own home and tried to get them to come over, rather than leave the house.

Ironically, now that I'd been required to stay inside, I wanted nothing more than to get out.

The Tesla called to me from the parking structure below, beckoning me, silently begging to be set free for a quick spin. It was dark now, so no one would see me. I'd take her out, just for a few minutes, and come right back. Easy.

A snicker escaped me at the image of Jackie driving my car after being so spoiled with hers. Well, she'd been the one to insist on switching cars, just like we'd switched IDs. I grabbed my baseball cap, pulled it low over my forehead and plucked Jackie's keys off the hook by the door.

Getting caught wasn't an option, not without Stella around to bail me out. Keeping my head down, I opened the door and hurled myself past the threshold, into the hallway — and slammed into a chest. A very big, firm chest.

"Holy broken nose, Batman." My nose burned and I squeezed my eyes shut as they stung in pain.

"In a hurry?" the owner of the hard chest said. I knew that voice...

I lifted my chin to meet his gaze and stared into familiar charcoal gray eyes. "I — "

Dallas Bines.

Jackie's ex.

My dream crush.

My mouth dropped open. An image flashed through my mind of the last article I'd read called *Top Ten Hollywood Abs*. They'd given him the number three spot, but in my opinion, he should've rated first. No contest.

"Are you okay?"

"Well, depends if you know a good surgeon." I may not have been obsessed with my looks like Jackie, but the less I resembled the elephant man, the happier I'd be. I covered my nose with my hand. If I did look grotesque, I didn't want *Dallas Bines* to see.

Dallas laughed softly. "I'm sure it's fine. Let me have a look."

He laid a steadying hand on my elbow and his other hand gently pried my fingers from my face. His hands were warm and soothing and my resistance melted away.

Oh, my God. Dallas Bines, the object of my two-year obsession was actually *touching* me. My nerve endings pulsed at his nearness and I tried to ignore how his gray eyes seemed to see through me. He looked different in the flesh. His hair wasn't as dark, only a shade lighter than mine. But he was just as gorgeous as in the magazines. Maybe even more so.

Already, the pain was subsiding which pushed me toward the theory that nothing was broken. That didn't mean my face wouldn't be bruised tomorrow for the premier. I hoped Stella had arranged a miracle worker to do my makeup.

His one hand remained at my elbow and the other cupped my cheek. He leaned toward me for a closer look. "Your nose looks the same as before."

Suddenly thirsty, I licked my lips. "I think I'm good. Feels better now."

"On your way somewhere?" The gravelly tone of his voice commanded me to freeze.

Not that I was about to move any time soon. It was as if an invisible string connected me to him. Oh, wait. He was still holding my face and my elbow. He really needed to stop being so hot while his hands were on me.

"Uh, I was about to go for a drive," I said, trying to ignore the pressure of his thumb at my elbow.

"In sweats?" His gaze traveled from my waist to my tennis shoes. A smile spread over his face. "I don't think I've ever seen you without super high heels. Didn't realize how short you are."

I fought back a blush, feeling like I'd just been thoroughly dissected. Jackie never blushed. I'd already risked exposing myself to the first person I ran into.

"Are you sick or something?" he asked as his hand slid down my arm to my fingers. "You look flushed."

This was getting worse. I swallowed, which made me feel even thirstier as I tried to come up with a reply that sounded like Jackie, but my mouth went numb.

I forced a smile. "I'm fine. Didn't plan on getting out of the car, so I figured no one would notice."

His brows furrowed. "Since when does Jackie Bloom go out for leisurely drives without being seen by someone? Isn't the whole point of leaving the house to attract attention? Where are you really going?" He gave me a crooked smile.

"Uhm." My front teeth grazed my lower lip.

Leaving the condo had been a horrible idea. If I didn't stop talking immediately, Dallas would discover I was an imposter. Stella wouldn't get her bonus and Jackie would be forced to come back.

Dallas's eyes crinkled at the corners and I wondered what it would feel like to run my fingers through his hair. I had to snap out of it, because I shouldn't want to date ex-boyfriends of sisters or friends. Ever. Besides, he'd already dumped me. Dumped Jackie, I mean. Whatever. Point was, even if he became interested in Jackie again, which he wouldn't, he'd be bored out of his mind with Jackie's country-girl twin.

I inched my hand away, but his fingers tangled with mine. A delicious shiver ran up my spine.

Dallas Bines was off limits, I reminded myself.

"I need to go rest my nose." Without another word, I spun on my sneaker, breaking his hold on my hand, and took the two steps back to my door. I reached for the knob, then glanced over my shoulder. Dallas looked baffled... but gorgeously so.

I vanished into my temporary home, resolved never again to leave it without Stella.

~~~

After what felt like hours in the chair the next day getting a make-over, I squirmed in the back seat of the limo, thankful that Jackie and I had similar metabolisms. The most beautiful dress I'd ever seen fit me to perfection. Its smooth lines of silver satin fabric hugged my waist, then draped elegantly over my hips. I felt like a princess. More accurately, I felt like a movie star. After a couple hours in skyscraper heels, however, I'd feel pain.

Stella leaned forward and adjusted a bobby pin, securing a lock of my hair. "I outdid myself. You look amazing."

"I think you missed your calling," I said. "Why not do hair and makeup for a living?"

She shrugged. "I'm always afraid it won't be as much fun if I'm depending on it to pay the rent."

I'd planned on doing the same as Stella, so how could I fault her? Instead of following my passion, photography, I'd checked out colleges to study business management. Maybe I'd have to rethink that…

"What's the name of the movie we're seeing?" I asked, amazed Stella hadn't already filled me in on the players. Or maybe she had. Too much information had been crammed into my head and since the run-in with Dallas I couldn't keep anything straight.

"Mistaken Identity." Stella smirked.

"You're kidding, right?" Talk about ironic.

Stella held back a giggle. "Tommy Landers plays two guys who look exactly alike and eventually switch places. They fall for each other's girlfriends and mess up each other's lives. It's a romantic comedy."

"How well does Jackie know Tommy?" I jolted when Stella's hand shot out to grab my wrist before I could rub my eye.

"Try not to ruin your makeup." She plucked a tiny mirror from her purse and handed it to me.

By then, the itch had faded, so I returned the mirror to Stella. It was going to be a long night if I couldn't scratch like normal people.

She leaned back again and crossed her legs. "Tommy played her boyfriend in *A Time for Courage* about a year ago. It's still in post-production. Anyway, they hate each other, so feel free to ignore him. Jackie always does."

If only I could ignore everyone else, too. "Unless someone comes by with a camera, right? Then I act like we're best buddies."

Stella chuckled. "You're catching on."

The closer we got to the theater, the more my adrenalin pumped. I slowly sucked in a breath, hoping my hands would stop trembling.

"You really need to change your face," Stella said, folding her arms over her chest and staring me down.

"That would defeat the whole purpose of this impersonation, wouldn't it?" I asked.

"No, I mean that grim expression. Like someone's holding a gun to your head." Stella clicked her tongue.

"I feel like a fraud." I bit my lower lip and averted my eyes. "What do you say to snooty people who act like they're better than you? How do you deal with all this and not go crazy?"

"My mom is Jackie's manager, so I grew up around her famous clients. One thing I've learned over the years, they're just people, Maddie. Celebrities still cheat on their spouses or end up in rehab. Being famous doesn't make you better than everyone else and don't let them convince you otherwise."

I ran an unsteady hand over the skirt of my gown. "I've been living in the country my whole life. I feel so out of place in the city."

"This world, and every city in it, belongs as much to you as it does to anybody. And no one has any power over you unless you give it to them." She gave me a soothing smile. "If *I* can handle these guys, so can you."

My mouth gaped. "Damn, you're good, Stella."

"I want you to rock that red carpet." She gave me a cocky grin, then swept her hand toward the tinted glass of the limo. "Here we are."

Wait. She wants *me* to rock the carpet. What about her? Dread washed over me. "You won't be with me?" I asked.

"I'm not famous and I'm not your date," Stella said, confirming my worst fear. "They don't want me there."

I groaned.

About half a block away, search lights lit up the outside of the theater. Enormous guys with shoulders stretched back, wearing solemn expressions and dark suits, sprinkled the sidelines and guarded the perimeter.

"When they're snapping pictures, do that smile we practiced when I was doing your makeup. Whatever you do, keep it up. Scowls look terrible on camera. Those bad photos are the ones they sell to the rags with captions like, 'Jackie Checks Into Rehab' or 'Jackie Dumped by Her Latin Lover.' So, no frowning, okay? Plus, it gives you wrinkles."

Geez, no wonder Jackie depended on her so much. "Stella, you totally deserve double whatever Jackie's paying you."

At the front of the line, a limo door opened and my pre-Dallas long-time crush, Luke Holtz, the star of Jackie's and my favorite TV show *Otherworld*, stepped out. He showed white teeth as cameras flashed, then he turned and offered an arm to a pretty blond girl who'd just emerged behind him.

In a matter of moments, that would be me posing. Except I'd do it alone. My stomach pinched.

"No need to panic," Stella said in a soft voice. "I called ahead and made it very clear that Jackie wasn't giving any interviews. All you have to do is walk and smile."

"Somehow, I don't think it's as easy as you make it out to be." My shoulder muscles tensed.

"You'll be fine. We're up next. I'll meet you at the other end." Stella gathered her purple, beaded gown closer to her body and scooted toward the back of the limo. The driver opened the door on my side and I moved to step out.

"Wait." She grasped my upper arm. "You have to pose for the photographers in front of the step and repeat, but just for a couple minutes, then you can move on."

"Step and what?" God, couldn't she have gone over this before the limo stopped? Butterflies waged war in my stomach.

"Step and repeat. The wall with the sponsors all over it, where you stand and they take your picture. You remember how to do the pose?"

I nodded. "Yeah, one foot in front of the other, bend the knee."

"Don't forget to do something with your arms." Stella nodded toward the door.

Oh, crap. I was really going to do this. "Got it," I said.

As delicately as I could, I stuck one leg out then the other, the glare from the lights nearly blinding me after being in the dark limo. I stood up and mustered all my will to smile, then took a step forward, keeping my eye on the other end of the long, red path.

Oh, Lord, how did Jackie walk in stilettos when she had so many hours in them? I shouldn't have let Stella talk me out of my sneakers. Even a pair of boots would have been better. It's not like anyone could see my shoes under the yards of shimmering silver fabric cascading around my feet.

As if the shoes weren't dangerous enough, I had to worry about tripping over my own dress. I wanted to rush past the press line, but my shoes and dress prevented it. Maybe I could save time by cutting the step and repeat short.

What was Jackie thinking to choose a dress, no matter how gorgeous, with no straps? It looked great on or off the hanger, but horrifyingly, it felt like it was slipping. I snuck a discreet peek only to find my dress hadn't budged.

And don't get me started on the fake eyelashes. Sure, they looked great on camera, but the glue felt weighty on my lids every time I blinked. At least they toned down my wide-eyed look of terror, giving me a sultry bedroom look.

A few more steps and I hit the carpet. It had a wide sponsor board on one side and on the other side was a three-foot deep line of press all crowding together for the best shot. Cameras clicked and people shouted out my sister's name. Keeping my distance from them, I stopped, pasted on a smile and struck the pose Stella had taught me.

A part of me was just a little bit dazzled by the glamour. How many people could say they'd walked a red carpet filled with A-list celebrities? My friend Angie would just die if she knew what I was doing. Still, I wouldn't be sad when the whole thing was finished and my feet were flat again.

I continued walking, then paused again to pose — shoulders back, chin up, big smile, knee bent. But my gaze wandered. As much as I hated playing Jackie, I was thrilled to recognize some of the actors. My eyes devoured the familiar faces, like Luke Holtz who smiled at his date, then turned back to say something to the interviewer. She threw her head back and laughed. Several other stars were speaking with the press as well, like Lazarus Mayer from *Dark of Night*, another of my favorite shows.

"Jackie, over here." A man's camera clicked. When I rotated, there were a series of clicks from others behind the press line. In my peripheral, a couple walked toward the step and repeat — my cue to pass the spotlight to the next person.

The red carpet part was almost over.

A short man in a suit leaned over the rope and yelled something as he stretched his microphone toward me. I backed up and continued walking with a powerful urge to move faster gripping me. Dutifully, I paused again a few feet later and repeated the pose.

"Jackie, how do you plan to get Henley to cast you?" a woman asked, followed by a man asking, "Do you think you've got a shot at playing Amy?"

Well trained by Stella, I just kept up my smile. In a hurry to move on, I quickly twisted around and crashed into a rock-hard human-filled tuxedo. I thrust a leg back for equilibrium, but stepped on my dress and lost my balance.

I was about to go down — in front of probably hundreds of people. Oh, god, I'd die of embarrassment before my butt ever hit the ground.

Just before I descended, a pair of strong hands grasped my waist from behind me. "I gotcha," he said, holding me steady, then he stepped away. An instant later, he was smiling for the cameras and speaking into a microphone as if he hadn't just taken a moment to save me from humiliation. Dallas Bines.

Dallicious Bines would be a more fitting name.

Anxious to get the carpet walk over with, I forged on, praying I'd survive the rest of Jackie's gig without breaking my neck. Thankfully, I made it to the end of the step and repeat in one piece where Stella waited for me wearing a proud grin.

"I almost ate it on the carpet. Did you see?" I asked in a hushed voice.

"Didn't notice at all. I doubt anyone else did either. You looked like a pro out there, a natural."

Yeah, naturally awkward. "My feet are killing me, Stella. Can we go someplace to rest them?"

"There's a lounge upstairs where we can chill until the movie starts. We've got balcony seats and there's a bathroom close by. Walking should be minimal the next little while."

"Oh, thank God," I said.

"Stop fidgeting." Stella gave me a stern look. "Jackie never gets twitchy. Ever. Oh, crap. Luke's coming this way. Don't worry. You've never met him—but you're about to."

I could do this.

"Hi. Luke Holtz, big fan." He held out his hand and gave me a big smile, full of beautiful, white teeth. "This is my sister, Heather."

My whole body filled with rapture at the thought of having a conversation with him. But I was supposed to be Jackie, not some fan-girl. Lifting my chin, I smiled, but kept it conservative—as if I met huge stars like him every day. "Nice to meet you both. Love your show," I said, keeping my tone light.

His blond head whipped around when his name was called from near the door to the theater. "I'm needed," he said. "I'll see you later?"

"You know it." I smiled again and he strolled away.

"Luke seems interested in you. I probably don't need to remind you what a good idea it is to avoid him. Everyone, actually." Stella grabbed my hand. "But if someone manages to talk to you, just roll with it. Smile and comment on the weather. You'll be fine. Let's go."

As I followed her toward the front door of the theater, I spotted more press up ahead. We'd have to pass them to get inside. Just before the door, Stella shielded me and I slipped by the mob, only to come face-to-face with a microphone blocking my way to freedom.

"Jackie, our readers want to know who you're dating now. Rumor has it you've traded one musician for another."

That was a rumor Jackie would want stomped into itty bitty pieces. "I-I'm not currently dating anyone." I smiled politely, then darted around the reporter. Stepping through a doorway at least twice my height, I pivoted so my eyes could devour the stained glass above stretching to the ceiling. Over the threshold, I turned to gawk at the window, stepping aside so others could pass.

"I keep worrying someone's going to come along, someone who knows Jackie, who I have no info on. We should keep moving," Stella said for my ears only.

Oh, yes, way to relax me, Stella. I stiffened as she tugged on my arm.

"Besides," she continued, "you're acting like this is all new to you. Try being more aloof."

"I'm at a Hollywood premiere and I haven't fainted. I'd say I'm doing pretty good." I wasn't supposed to *appear* like a newbie though, so I'd work on that. I dragged my eyes from the stained glass, but they caught on the corbels momentarily as we passed through another doorway. The architecture of the building was stunning. I could stare at the decorative fixtures for hours and still not get to all of it.

Slowly, we wove through the throng of celebrities and schmoozers. People I didn't know, but recognized from movies smiled at me, nodded or waved as I passed. I followed their lead, matched their gestures, and kept moving. Just before the stairs, I saw Dallas. Of all people, he'd be hardest to avoid, since he and Jackie were friends and neighbors. And since they'd dated, he could easily discover I wasn't Jackie and expose me. I quickly glanced away just as his head snapped to me.

My face hurt from smiling and if one more person tried to photograph me, I'd be tempted to stab them with the heel of my shoe. They kept getting right in my face. Plus, I was absolutely positive that the layer of makeup on my face was bubbling, which didn't help my insecurities. But I forced my mouth to do the unnatural and curl up just a little while longer.

A few minutes later, Stella and I freshened up in the restroom with a few spare minutes before show time. As it turned out, the only thing bubbling had been my brain.

We claimed a settee in the long corridor near the entrance closest to our seats. As Stella advised, I faced her, so I couldn't see anyone approaching. They'd be more likely to keep walking if they thought we were deep in conversation.

Stella's gaze wandered to something behind me. "Oh, hell. Dallas Bines is coming our way. Keep it short and sweet while I figure out how to get away."

Chapter Three

My heart fluttered and I steeled myself not to get all warm and gooey over Dallas, a guy I barely knew.

"Hey, Stella, Jackie."

I shot him a smile over my shoulder, then turned back to Stella, hoping that would be enough for him.

Turned out.... not so much.

Next thing I knew, he was on my left, towering over Stella and me. Right then, I wished I had my camera. The photographer in me pictured Dallas wearing that sexy tux and leaning against a door frame, ankles crossed, a faraway look in his eyes, bow tie loosened and his hands stuffed in the pockets. Black and white, matte finish.

His weight rested on one leg, like he was in no hurry to leave. That pose would've made a great shot too. "How's your nose?" he asked.

"All good now. Thanks for asking. And thanks for the save out there." I gave him another smile, but it faltered when he narrowed his eyes ever so slightly.

"Dallas, what movie are you working on now?" Stella asked, jumping to my rescue.

"I'm between projects." His eyes flashed to mine. "I'm home a lot these days."

Stella gave a nervous giggle. "That's great."

Oh, geez, if Stella buckled in his presence, how could I be expected to do any better?

Damn, he smelled good. A little bit musky and a whole lot of yum.

Dallas nodded, his gaze steady on me. "Maybe I could switch seats with Stella and she could sit with my brother. You remember, Dave, don't you, Stella? He's been asking about you."

"Uh…" Her words stuck in her throat and, for a moment, she seemed torn.

"Stella and I are going over some things." I opened my tiny purse and pretended to look through it. "Privately. Maybe next time?"

Dallas's brows lowered as he studied me. "You two are up to something. You're both acting weird. You," he aimed an index finger at me, "especially."

"Ha," I scoffed. "It's business as usual. We just have a lot going on."

"I'm not buying it." One corner of his mouth curved up. "You're sitting with me."

My jaw went slack as I stared at him, unsure how to respond. If I said no, would he become even more suspicious? Plus, my resistance was breaking down. I mean, hello? I'd crushed on him for years and here he was asking me to sit next to him in the dark. How much did Jackie expect me to take?

Stella gave a nervous laugh. "Jackie and I are working."

"Now?" He shook his head. "Come on."

"Sure, if it makes you happy," I told Dallas, trying to convince myself that giving in to his request was only to keep up the charade. Jackie was Stella's boss. I needed to act like it. Right? "You and I can go over that stuff later."

Stella looked panicked, but what choice did I have?

He pressed his lips into a straight line, like he was suppressing a smile, and offered his arm. "You look beautiful tonight."

I stood and slipped my arm through his. "Thank you. You look…" Dallicious? I couldn't say that. "Good too."

He chuckled as we entered the theater. Oh, Lord, he had a sexy voice, all low and growly.

Once we found our seats, Stella's gaze followed the direction of Dallas's index finger. A slightly older version of Dallas waved from a seat near the next aisle over.

"I'll go around to the other entrance." Stella's lips thinned to a straight line and her eyes gave me the silent message, *Don't say too much*, then she took off.

Why did Dallas want to sit next to Jackie anyway? Was he interested? Hadn't he already been there and dumped that? This made me wonder how serious Jackie and Dallas had been. I'd never gotten the details, just the glossy version. Did they have sex? I immediately ejected that image from my head.

As soon as we'd taken our seats, Dallas twisted to face me. "Everything going okay?"

"Of course." I unfolded my hands to make a production out of straightening my dress.

"You're not fooling me, you know."

"What do you mean?" My entire body tensed.

"Shh!" He held a finger to his lips as the lights dimmed and the screen lit up, saving me from his scrutiny. I crossed my arms over my chest and vowed to ignore Mr. Hotness.

Yeah, like I could forget Dallas Bines was currently sitting right next to me in the dark.

I stared straight ahead, but the expression *out of sight, out of mind* meant nothing when I could still smell that clean, musky scent that made my mind go in forbidden directions.

Despite his broad shoulders and my constant struggle not to rest my head on one of them, I managed to catch snippets of the movie. It was a romantic comedy, which was usually my thing when I didn't have certain distractions…

An hour and forty-five minutes later, the credits rolled over the giant screen, lights flooded the theater. As soon as I could get away, I needed to find Stella and, hopefully, get the hell out of there.

"What did you think?" he asked.

"It was great." I grinned.

He gave me a skeptical glance. "Really? I thought

you didn't like chick flicks. You always go for the action packed movies." He turned toward me, his arm brushing against mine. A little shiver skated along my skin. "You're full of surprises today," he said.

"No, not really." I should have made my excuse and left, but I was frozen in my seat with my heart pounding wildly from his touch. Help! Where was Stella? A chill vibrated through me and I held my arms.

"Here." He stood, then shrugged out of his jacket and turned it so the jacket lining faced me.

I rose to slip an arm into one sleeve, then turned as he slid the fabric over my other arm and past my shoulders. His musky scent wafted from the fabric and invaded my brain. Involuntarily, I bent my head and inhaled. I faced him again, but he hadn't let go of the jacket, which left me uncomfortably close to him.

"What game are you playing?" he asked.

The metaphoric gun clicked at my temple. "What do you mean?"

"C'mon. You know what I'm talking about." It was almost a whisper, but not like he was the bad guy cornering me. He sounded…concerned. And very nice.

Nice. That's how Jackie had described Dallas when she'd said he wasn't her type. Well, if *nice* meant incredibly sexy, sweet and confident, *nice* was definitely a good thing to me. A very good thing.

Uh…what was his question?

"We'll talk about it over a drink," he said when I didn't answer.

I swallowed. If he knew Jackie well enough — and I was struggling not to think about the two of them *really* getting to know each other — given enough time, he'd figure out that I definitely was not Jackie. My head reeled with various scenarios of us having drinks together and me giving myself away. Every ounce of me wanted to say yes, but it could ruin Jackie if he discovered the truth.

He motioned for me to go first and I led the way from the balcony section and into the second floor lobby. We took the elevator down to the first floor, but could barely push through the mass of schmoozing people.

The giant chandelier above cast light on the women showing off their sparkling gowns. Cameras flashed as the media captured the various celebrities in natural situations — and I use the term *natural* hesitantly considering how acutely aware they all were of their bodies and what positions flattered them most.

How would Stella find me amidst the throng of people? Because of Dallas's height, he'd stand out. But if Stella only saw his back, he'd look like a lot of other guys in a dark suit.

My skin tingled when Dallas's hand closed around mine and we squeezed through the crowd. He stopped on the other side of the large room where a few inches of free space opened up.

A waiter appeared in front of me, but I hardly noticed as my focus remained fixed on Dallas. I hoped I successfully hid my fascination over his masterfully chiseled features. And that little smile that reached his eyes. Totally swoon-worthy.

Dallas was only around twenty. He gave the impression he'd packed a lot into a short time. With all that experience, would he be a good kisser?

I blushed when I caught myself focusing on his lips. He was talking. Oh, crap, I hadn't been paying attention.

"Jackie? Would you like a drink?" Dallas said, nodding toward the server who appeared to have said something to me. That same smile played at the corner of his mouth, like he had a secret.

My brain engaged again and I gawked at the server. "I'm not drinking. Besides, I'm not twenty-one."

The waiter's blond brows flew up and I wondered what I'd said wrong.

"Really?" a woman asked behind my shoulder. "Jackie Bloom has given up drinking? That can't be."

Apparently, my brain wasn't fully up and running or I would've just accepted the glass. I didn't have to drink from it. I twisted around to see a redheaded woman with an extremely smug look on her face. Did Jackie know her?

"Lisa Alcott, *Exposed Magazine*." Instead of reaching out for a hand shake, her green eyes narrowed. "What would make you give up alcohol?"

"I…I'm not in the mood tonight," I said. *Exposed* was the worst of them all, constantly printing retractions or getting sued. They probably kept printing trash because they sold enough papers to make up for it. Forget the truth.

Lisa's cat-like smile grew wider with each second. "Hm."

I sucked at impersonating Jackie. I'd make a horrible actress. And I couldn't help wondering how much my little sister — by two minutes — drank when she went to these events. I forged on, adding a little snark like I'd seen Jackie do. "It's not mandatory, is it?"

"No, but you're not exactly known for your discretion."

Witch. "You don't have many friends, do you?" I asked.

She'd already sidled up to Dallas as though she hadn't heard me.

"Are you two back together?" she asked him, then her eyes strayed to my shoulders. "Nice jacket."

Oh, yeah. It totally looked like we were dating.

"Lisa, I promise you Jackie and I are just friends. There's no story here."

"You're hiding something." Lisa folded her arms over her chest and smirked.

"You're wasting your time with us, Lisa." Dallas grabbed my hand and led me away. Realizing that Lisa was right behind us, he stopped short of the door and whirled around. "Have a good night."

She scowled, probably because all her baiting hadn't gotten either of us to slip. But she didn't need our cooperation. She'd probably use the pictures of Dallas and me together to make up a story, simply be-cause that was her job — to twist the truth and create controversy. I'd heard enough rumors about Jackie to know I should never take anything at face value. But other readers may not see through the lies.

"Let's go." He tugged on my hand again, compelling me to trail after him.

Although I wanted to go with him, the sane part of me knew this was a bad idea. Where was Stella? I glanced back, but didn't see her. Dallas stopped just outside the back door. My gaze drifted to a group huddled several yards away and the cloud of smoke around them. The smoking section.

Lisa hadn't followed us outside, probably because she'd already gotten what she needed. Dread settled in my stomach. Jackie was supposed to be on sabbatical. She didn't need to read a bunch of garbage about herself while she was still recovering from her previous humiliation. I glanced at Dallas.

He was staring at me. "That was odd."

Oh, geez, what had I done?

"You know they wouldn't serve a minor here. Or was that just a clever way of getting attention?"

Oh, crap. Of course they wouldn't serve me with the press around. Worse, while I was being an idiot, I confirmed what a media whore Jackie was.

"C'mon. You're going to pretend you've never been served in a public place before?" I lifted a careless shoulder.

"Not with the press around."

This impersonation gig couldn't end soon enough for me. Life was much easier when I could just be myself. Except then I wouldn't see Dallas again.

"So I forgot myself for a moment." I rolled my eyes. Acting was kind of like lying. I felt bad deceiving Dallas, but isn't that why I was there?

"Well, Lisa won't see it that way. She'll put a crazy spin on you refusing a drink, along with some trashy speculation. It'll probably get picked up in every tabloid across the country."

"Does that kind of stuff ever bother you?" I asked, overlapping the lapels of his jacket against the chill night air and tucking myself into the fabric.

He held his arms close to his sides and stuffed his hands in his pockets. "Not tonight. You?"

"It's expected, right? Without publicity, an actor's career could die. Goes with the job." A generic enough reply while not really answering the question. I felt uneasy blatantly lying to Dallas and needed to keep it to a minimum.

"It sure does." He studied me a moment. "Do you want to go back inside?"

Jackie would say yes. Not me. I'd shown up at the premier and that's all that was required. My job was done. "No. You?"

"Not really. Are you hungry?"

I knew I shouldn't say it, but… "Starving. Haven't eaten all day. I was afraid the dress wouldn't fit right and I didn't want to feel fat when I had to look good."

"It's great to be a guy." He flashed me a smile. "Did you drive here with Stella?"

Stella. I kept forgetting about her. "Yes."

"Why don't you leave the limo for her and I'll drive you home?" He grinned. "Since I'm going there anyway."

He was impossible to resist. But he was my sister's ex. Forbidden territory. Going there was not a reality for me, no matter how fab he looked in a tux. But I rationalized that we already knew he wasn't interested in Jackie. He'd even made that clear to Lisa. What kind of trouble could I possibly get into? Dallas would drive me home and we'd say goodnight.

"Sure. I'll just text her and let her know the car's all hers." I reached into my purse to grab my cell. Four texts had come in, all from Stella. If I hadn't turned my ringer off during the movie, I would've heard the alerts.

The first text, Stella said she was sorry for allowing Dave to distract her and that she was looking for me. Knowing now what Dave looked like, it was easy to imagine how he could delay a girl. The next three texts wondered where I was, each more hysterical than the last.

"New phone?" He nodded toward it, smirking. "Or should I say *old* phone? Downgraded, huh?"

Oops. Right. Jackie and I hadn't switched phones.

"The other one was acting up, so I had them connect to this one until Stella could sort it out." I returned to texting Stella, hoping he bought my lie. Lies would be so much easier to avoid if I walked away and drove home with Stella. But I'd already committed...

My cell phone vibrated and I checked the text. Stella again. *Don't go a/where with him. 2 risky. Where r u?*

I glanced at Dallas and the thrumming in my veins reaffirmed my decision.

It was just dinner.

Leaving the volume down, I closed my phone and dropped it in my purse. "Let's go."

Chapter Four

As Dallas backed his black, Mercedes SUV out of the parking spot, I retrieved my phone and replied to Stella. *Sorry. Already gone. Dallas will drop me off.*

It vibrated again seconds later. *Are you INSANE??!! Stop the car! I'll pick u up wherever u r. Say u hv a headache, say ANYTHING. Just get out of the car!*

Too late now. Sorry! I typed back. I bit my lip, suppressing a smile. I wasn't big on breaking rules. What had I been thinking in saying yes? Maybe Jackie's personality was rubbing off on me. *I'll c u in the a.m.*

After a long silence, a new text came in. *Tmrw is Sat. U hv that gig @ 2. I will b there @ 12 sharp & help u get ready. If I still hv a job by then....* As soon as I finished reading it, another text appeared. *U better not blow my bonus.*

I probably *would* blow it with Dallas. Obviously, the more time I spent with him, the greater the chance of him catching on — if he hadn't already. But something in my gut told me that Dallas wasn't the kind of guy who'd sell me out.

And didn't I deserve one nice meal for all my hard work on the red carpet?

"Why didn't you arrive in a limo like everyone else?" I asked.

"I prefer driving over being a passenger," he said, glancing at me as I dropped the phone back into my purse. "You seem better. I'm glad. I know how hard it's been for you lately. People don't recover from that kind of thing overnight."

The married guy, of course. But I didn't want to go there, since I'd never even met Pete. Instead, I just nodded.

We went to one of those cute little sidewalk cafés on Franklin, close to our building. Everyone stared as the hostess seated us at a table in the corner where we weren't as conspicuous. Like that was even possible the way we were dressed.

Crowded white-clothed tables surrounded us and waiters bustled, weaving between customers. Several girls slightly younger than me giggled at the curb and pointed at Dallas. But the chaos of the restaurant, and the passing cars just yards away, deterred them from approaching us. Fine by me. I wanted him all to myself.

A few minutes later, a waitress with dark, spiky hair stood by our table and took our order. He ordered a burger with fries and I chose the garlic roasted chicken.

"Where's the restroom?" I asked Dallas.

He narrowed his eyes. "We've eaten here before."

Oops. "Extreme hunger is draining my brain." I lifted one bare shoulder and gave him my best helpless-damsel look.

He didn't look any less suspicious. "All the way in the back, take a right."

I left and, a few minutes later, made my way back to Dallas and the chair across from him.

He greeted me with a smile. "Two things women can always depend on at those red carpet events. Sore feet and starvation."

"No kidding." I giggled.

Our waitress set a basket of bread on the table, along with our entrees, then hurried off.

"That was fast." Dallas leaned sideways and reached under the table out of my line of vision. A moment later, his warm hands wrapped around my ankle. Gently, he slipped off one shoe, then the other. "Better?"

Too much better. Seeing him all sweet and considerate made him a real person. Someone I could actually fall for in more than a crush way.

Oh, God.

I would not fall for this guy. I had to shake it off. Just had to.

"Thank you." Stella was right. Hanging out with him had been a bad idea. Even knowing Stella would pick me up in a heartbeat, I couldn't make myself leave.

I took a bite of my garlic roasted chicken with renewed determination not to let myself develop any more feelings for Dallas than I already had. But while I was there, no harm in learning more about him.

"If you weren't an actor, what would you be?" I asked between bites.

"Acting is all I ever wanted to do." He lifted his glass for a sip of water.

That's how I felt about photography. But it was more practical to get a degree in something else, so I had a career to fall back on. "You must've thought about it," I said. "What else would you do? Back-up career."

"Hm." He tore a piece from his garlic bread and popped it in his mouth. "I didn't see my older sister for a year. She came back when she was seventeen to drop her baby off with my parents, then she took off again. A couple years later, I started hanging out with these guys and getting into trouble. My parents decided to send me to military camp, rather than watch me follow in my sister's footsteps."

"I guess it worked. Unless you have a kid some-where no one knows about," I joked.

"No kids. Just my niece I told you about." He smiled. "She's adorable."

With Dallas's shared genes, she had to be super cute.

"Anyway, it might be cool to run a camp where troubled kids could work with horses, learn how to fish, hike, maybe build things. I loved it when I went. Straightened me out. Put things in perspective for me. If my sister had something like that back then, maybe little Bridget would have a mom right now."

Apparently, Jackie hadn't met Bridget yet, which made it safe to ask questions. "When was the last time you saw her?" I asked.

"Last weekend, we went to Disneyland."

I'd meant his sister, but I loved how his eyes lit up talking about his niece, so I kept quiet. "I bet she loved that. It's so magical when you're a kid."

"We had a blast. She's five now and she's got this big head of curly, black hair and dimples. And, man, you'd be amazed how much kids can talk when they have a captive audience."

I laughed. "Just the two of you went to Disneyland?"

"Yeah. I told her it was Uncle/Niece day. You gonna finish that?" He pointed at my plate.

His devotion as an uncle made me all warm and squishy inside. That he loved her enough to endure a full day with crowds and squealing kids left me speechless. I shook my head and slid my plate across the table.

"So your next movie, what's it about?" I asked.

A slow smile spread over his face. "Chick flick. Not for you."

If he only knew how much I loved the girly movies. "I always wonder why guys do those when they don't even like them."

"That's like wondering why a chef cooks meat if he's a vegetarian. Or why a jeweler sells diamonds if she prefers rubies. It's part of the business and it was a good script. I don't watch my own movies anyway."

After the comment on the jewelry, I barely heard anything else. Why not used cars or something? Did he suspect that my summer job was really at a jewelry store? It was a quick reminder who I really was and that this dinner was all pretend.

He ate the last bite of my chicken and set the fork down.

Time to go. I patted my lips with the linen napkin. "We should probably head home."

Dallas rotated his wrist to glance at his watch. "Kind of early to call it a night. For you anyway."

As appealing as it was to hang out with Dallas a little longer, it was way past my bedtime and I didn't want to get so exhausted that I completely forgot to be Jackie. "Maybe I'm unpredictable." I scrunched up my nose and grinned.

"I'm beginning to see that," he said.

My insides fluttered uncontrollably. Despite my vow that this was just dinner, I fell for him just a little more.

~~~

A half hour later, evil stilettos in hand, I exited the elevator and onto the floor of our building.

"I like you without those heels."

"You mean you like me super short?" I smiled up at Dallas. He was a foot taller than me, which put him about six-two. I didn't necessarily like it when guys towered over me, because it made me feel even shorter than I already was. But on him, I didn't care. He was exactly right just the way he was.

"I like you either way." He stopped in front of his door. "Coffee?"

Coffee inside his place? I halted mid-step and whirled around to stand right in front of him. My mouth opened, but words warred with the will of my tongue.

"What's wrong?" he asked.

"Dallas, what are we doing? You wanted to stop seeing her...I mean me, remember? So what's all this jacket offering and dinner business about?"

"Hey." He brushed a finger under my chin. "It's just coffee."

Except that the way he touched me didn't feel like *just coffee*. It felt more like *come inside and we'll brew up something hot.* "If that's the case, then maybe we should do it *not* in your home."

"Deal. We'll go to Anna's Café. They have great pancakes. Around nine tomorrow morning then?" His brows rose as he waited for my answer.

Maybe he was just one of those guys who touched a lot, but didn't mean anything by it. I shouldn't read anything into his gestures. Breakfast was probably just a buddy thing for him. That was for the best, right?

"Sure. See you then." I spun and made a dash for my door—before I let myself believe that maybe he liked me more than just a friend. Getting involved with him would be a road to disaster.

~~~

Waking with a jolt, I immediately glanced next to me. The silk sheets on the other side of the bed were smooth and the pillow fluffed. No one had been there.

But in my dream, Dallas had come to tell me how much he loved me. He'd carried me into the bedroom and gently laid me down. Then I'd awoken without getting that kiss or anything else. Probably my subconscious telling me it wasn't going to happen. Ever.

Future or not, I couldn't stop thinking about him — the gray of his eyes and the subtle hint of beard that had begun forcing its way out by the time he'd dropped me off the night before.

It wasn't just his looks that gave him power over my brain. Looks didn't mean much — as I'd found out when I'd dated Tyler the quarterback during my senior year, and Adam who I'd met last summer. Adam had floppy hair and the sexiest dimples I'd ever seen. Those guys weren't half as captivating as Dallas. For one thing, neither had gazed at me the way Dallas did.

Lending me his jacket so I wouldn't be cold, making sure I got something to eat after the premier, taking off my shoes at the restaurant and rubbing my feet, being madly in love with his five year old niece — yum.

Yep, I'd gone from infatuation over a fantasy to a huge crush. I couldn't let it turn into anything deeper. I'd make breakfast quick. Get in. Get out.

Half expecting to hear my parents chattering as my mom made breakfast, I yawned and stretched. I missed them. Living alone wasn't my thing at all.

With an hour and a half to kill before our break-fast *appointment*—not date—I could indulge for a bit, maybe grab some orange juice and read the newspaper in bed. Jackie liked to keep up on current events. At the very least, the papers would get a quick scan. She probably had them delivered.

I stretched my barely-there tank top down past my waist and stepped onto the cool wood floor.

I opened the door to the hallway and jumped at the sight of Dallas reaching down to pick up the newspaper in front of his door. I had a vague awareness of dark, messy hair, but was too distracted by his bare chest.

"Good morning." His gaze lowered to my tank top, then lowered still to my teeny tiny shorts.

He gave me a lopsided smile. "I'm glad you're up. We can do breakfast now."

The twinkle in his eyes commanded me to smile back. I couldn't help it. "Just rolled out of bed."

"I can see that." His eyes swept over me. "You should roll around in your bed more often."

"Um..." Lord, what the hell was he trying to do? The only image going through my mind was *him* rolling around in my bed. He was already dressed for it too—flannel boxers and nothing else. I pushed away the image of his arms wrapped around me and dropped my gaze to my toes, so he wouldn't see the heat rushing into my cheeks.

"Change of plans," he said. "We're doing breakfast at my place."

Chapter Five

"*Breakfast here? Anna's* delivers?" I asked, angling myself with my arms crossed over my chest so I didn't feel as naked.

"No. I'm cooking."

Dallas cooked? Another thing to add to my long list of what made him desirable. "You sure?"

"Absolutely." His eyes strayed to my tank top before meeting mine again. "Go get dressed and come over in twenty minutes." He turned to go, then paused. "On second thought, what you're wearing is just fine."

When I raised one brow, he shrugged and then went into his condo.

After brushing my teeth, I raced to Jackie's closet. Hopefully, she'd have something appropriate for a stay-in breakfast. Something that didn't require stilettos.

My eyes scanned the selection of skirts, tops and pants in every color and style, then landed on the shelves lined with boots. I breathed a sigh of relief when I found some with less than four inch heels.

The weatherman had warned that the temperature would reach the mid-eighties later. Grabbing a pair of jeans riddled with holes, I sifted through Jackie's blouses until I found a sleeveless top—something that covered more than what I'd worn to bed, but still kept me cool.

As I opened my front door, the scents of bacon and herbs hit me. My stomach growled. Well, no wonder it was so strong in the corridor—he'd left his door open.

"Dallas?" I called out.

"Come on in," he returned.

My cell vibrated, just as I pushed the door open the rest of the way. I dug it out of my pocket. Jackie. She was probably checking in. "I gotta take this. Be right back."

"Hey." I ducked back out into the hallway.

"Why are you whispering?" she asked.

I closed his door and raised my voice. "I'm not."

"Everything okay? You haven't run into any trouble, have you?"

"Uh…no."

"Uh-huh." Long pause, like she didn't believe a word of it. Even though, technically, I'd only uttered two.

"What's going on?" I asked, unable to fathom what could possibly be annoying her.

She exhaled. Loudly. "Did you see this morning's TMZ blog?"

Oops. Lisa's handi-work? "No. Why?"

"They're saying I'm pregnant, because I refused a

drink last night. What gives? You're young and single. Would it have killed you to imbibe?"

"I'm not twenty-one. Besides, lots of people don't drink," I said.

"But I do—until last night. Therefore, I must be knocked up," Jackie growled. "Worse, they're saying Dallas is the father and we're back together. The pictures of you wearing his jacket, then leaving together didn't help. Maddie, am I back together with Dallas?"

"Wh-What? No!"

"Did he drive you home last night?"

"Well..."

"Oh, my God." Her voice had taken on an apathetic tone, like I'd disappointed her. Hey, I was in this mess because I was doing her a favor. "Did you sleep with him?" she asked.

I straightened my spine, even though I knew she couldn't see over the phone. "No way. I just met him yesterday."

She sighed. "Out of all the reasons you could give me for not sleeping with him, *that's* the one you picked. How about — "

"One more minute." I held up an index finger when Dallas poked his head through the doorway.

"You're with him right now, aren't you? Oh, Maddie."

"He's just making me breakfast. No big deal."

She groaned. "He's *cooking* for you?"

I removed the phone from my ear. "It's a harmless

breakfast."

"Nothing harmless about what he whips up. His parents are chefs, so he's picked up a few tips and anything he makes is beyond yummy."

"Uhm, you're not doing a good job talking me out of it," I said.

"You know what I mean. Better to just avoid the whole package."

I snuck back into Jackie's condo, so I wouldn't have to worry about Dallas overhearing. "Hmmm."

"So you'll cancel breakfast, right?" It was more like a command than a request.

The scent of whatever delicious goodness he was whipping up followed me inside. Yeah…like I could turn that down. "But I'm hungry," I said, almost whining.

"Listen to me. This is *my* life you're living. And I'm so grateful you're doing this, but I could give you a million reasons why you need to stay away from Dallas, the least of all being that I dated him. Just keep in mind that if you start something up, do anything with him, I'm going to have to dump him when I get back. You get that, don't you?"

"I guess." She was right. It was wrong to make her deal with something I started. Not only that, he thought I was Jackie. What would I do when it was time to go home? I couldn't tell him I'd been lying and pretending to be someone else. Oh, yeah, that would go over well.

My heart sank. Anything I did with Dallas would only end badly for me. I couldn't afford any entanglements.

"Hey, Maddie?" Jackie asked.

"Yeah?"

"Thanks again for doing this." Her tone softened. "I'm sorry if I sound bitchy. It's not your fault tabloids suck."

"No problem." I smiled into the phone.

"And I know it can't be easy for you there without Mom and Dad, without me. But it won't be forever, then you'll be home again." She paused. "Which is more reason not to start anything up with Dallas."

She made a good argument. I shouldn't have said yes to *coffee.* "Yeah."

"You're doing the right thing. He's good at being adorable and, next thing you know, you're watching a movie at his house, *snuggling.*"

Jackie made snuggling sound like it was right up there with cleaning toilets. "What's wrong with snuggling?" I asked.

"Nothing wrong if you're going to keep him. But you're not. Besides, we're eighteen. We don't want to get tied down with one guy. This is the time to make mistakes and experience life while we're young and can still get away with it."

I couldn't disagree more. And she wasn't getting away with it at all. Not if you read the tabloids and all their judgy comments. But I didn't want to go into all that with her right then.

"Speaking of getting away with things. You're doing okay as me?" I asked.

"Easiest acting job I've ever had." She laughed. "You live an easy life, Maddie. It's just what I needed."

I smiled into the phone. "You sound better."

"It's good to get away."

We hung up just as Dallas tapped at the door. "Jackie?"

I swung the door open and the aroma, stronger this time, invaded my nose and tickled my saliva glands. My mouth watered.

He grinned. "Breakfast is ready."

So was I.

For a home-cooked meal, nothing else. He'd never go for me. As if.

Breakfast. That's it.

"Great. I'm starving." I followed Dallas into the dining room where two plates sat on a table, filled with an omelet next to fried potatoes and bacon.

He pulled a chair out for me. "Going for a more natural look today?"

Damn. Back home, I usually skipped makeup, like now. But I was supposed to be Jackie Bloom. Dressing up was required, even if you never left the building.

"I didn't want breakfast to get cold," I offered.

"I like the natural look on you." But he still seemed suspicious.

"Food smells great." My olfactory system danced in anticipation. I sat and scooted the chair in, hoping if I ignored his doubtful stare, he'd forget all about the recent changes in Jackie.

One side of his mouth lifted. "Dig in."

"Mm," I said, chewing the first bite. Not being much of a cook, I couldn't identify the spices. I only knew they were exactly right, blending perfectly with the bell peppers, mushrooms and what tasted like pepper jack cheese. "This is delicious."

"I'm glad you like it." He paused a moment, still watching me. "Would you mind reading with me? After we eat," he said between bites.

"A book?" What an odd request.

Dallas chuckled. "No, a script."

"I thought you weren't doing anything for a few weeks."

He nodded. "Yeah, but I've got a small part on *Love and Loathing*."

I tilted my head, brows drawn. "That's a daytime soap." A definite step down from starring in block-buster movies.

"Yeah, but my mom is a huge fan. She hasn't missed a show in thirty years. I play a fitness trainer. One of my lines is 'Happy birthday, Rose.' That's my mom's name and it airs on her birthday. I'm keeping that gig quiet though, so she'll be surprised."

Unbelievably sweet. My insides turned to mush.

Jackie had said Dallas was too nice. I was beginning to understand why it hadn't worked out with them. She went through guys like a bulldozer and wasn't very *nice*. Plus, she had terrible taste in men. Usually.

"So you'll read with me?"

As if I could say no after telling me about his mom's birthday present. I'd read with Jackie before. It didn't require much acting. "Sure."

I rose to take my plate to the sink, then rinsed it off. I swung around to stick it in the dishwasher and bumped right into Dallas and his hard chest. He grasped my shoulders to steady me.

"Sorry." I tried to back up, but my butt hit the counter.

"For what?" If he moved any closer, our thighs would touch.

I blinked.

"What are you doing later today?" he asked.

That voice. Sometimes gravely. Sometimes just above a whisper. It turned all his words into something sexy, even though he couldn't mean *everything* that way.

"I have an appearance at two. Stella's coming over at noon."

"What's it for?"

I leaned my elbows on the counter to create some distance between us, then held my breath as he reached over to brush a finger across my chin.

"Crumb," he informed me.

"Oh."

"So, where's your appearance?" he asked again, his eyes roaming my face.

"Hollywood Boulevard. A restaurant some famous guy is opening." I knew the name of the movie star, but my mind drew a complete blank. Probably because Dallas's nearness was sucking out my brains cells, little by little. How was I expected to function with his full, luscious lips so close to mine?

He chuckled. "You mean Steve Heller."

"Yeah, that guy."

"And what are your plans tomorrow tonight?" Dallas reached up to rub a lock of my hair between his thumb and finger.

"Plans?" My mouth went dry. He stood way too close and my concentration slipped.

"You *always* have plans." His eyes caressed my face.

"Not tomorrow night." Somewhere deep in my soul, I knew that was the wrong answer. But when your brain stops working, telling the truth is so much easier.

"A friend told me that Josh Adams is jamming at Hanks Blues. It's supposed to be a surprise. Should be fun."

I nodded, since it was all I was capable of at the moment.

"We'll have dinner there. I'll pick you up at six."

Preventing Dallas from making another date with me would've been smart. The words hovered in my throat, but I couldn't force them out. Even if I didn't reject his offer, I needed to say *something*. Or, at the very least, finish cleaning up after breakfast. And yet, I couldn't move. I just stared into his eyes as they fixed on mine.

His gaze fell to my mouth, then he reached both

hands up to cup my face and, inch by inch, lowered his mouth to mine.

Chapter Six

Our lips touched, feather-light. He shifted his body and brought his thighs against mine, but he didn't deepen the kiss. He just skimmed the surface, gently teasing my mouth until my nerve endings hummed. Seconds stretched and my lungs stilled as I ached for more.

Then, slowly, he withdrew, keeping close enough that I still felt his warm breath against my skin.

A thick haze clouded my brain and I worried he might ask me something, anything, that required a response and I'd slip up. I couldn't catch my breath. Fear that I'd blow it for Jackie paralyzed me.

Oh, my God! Jackie! If she knew I'd just kissed the guy who dumped her, she'd feel hurt and betrayed and what had we *just* talked about? Jackie didn't need this, on top of everything else.

"I..." I had no idea what to say. I only knew that if someone didn't say something soon and break the trance, I would let Jackie down worse than I already had. Because, more than anything, I wanted this guy, no matter how *nice* he was.

"Yes?" His gaze locked onto mine.

"You said it was just coffee."

He blinked.

"Last night, you assured me it was just coffee," I repeated.

An uncertain expression crossed his face. "I thought that at the time."

"But it should be. Just coffee, I mean," I whispered, as if saying it any louder would make the truth more painful and more real. I wanted to be with him, with nothing in our way. That wasn't going to happen though. "We've already been there, right?"

He stared at me, silent, like he couldn't quite go where I was trying to take him. Maybe he found it incomprehensible that a girl might say no to him.

"That's what my head keeps telling me," he said, brows drawn. "But I keep getting this feeling like we've just met and it's all new."

"You…" You what? You're right that I'm a liar and a fake?

He frowned and I inwardly cringed. I knew I should tell him right then and save him from the confusion he had to be feeling, but I chickened out. It wasn't my place to tell Jackie's secret and I'd made a promise.

"I can read those lines with you later. Stella will be here soon, so I should probably take off."

No idea if that was true or not, since I'd totally lost track of time and wasn't wearing my watch. I side-stepped and backed away.

"You're leaving?"

"Well, yeah. That appearance, remember?" Maybe he had intended to kiss me again. Maybe not. I wasn't going to stick around to find out.

He looked disappointed and I didn't want to come off bitchy. Not after he'd fed me, then laid dessert on me against the kitchen counter. So I slid my hand down his arm as I passed him — an intimate gesture while keeping my lips off him.

In the clear and a few feet away, I picked up my pace. "Thanks for the awesome breakfast," I threw over my shoulder.

"Sure. See you later."

Yes, he would. Tomorrow night. I shouldn't be thrilled at the thought of seeing him again, but I couldn't stifle it.

When I returned to my own life, I'd miss Dallas. There was something about him, something so not Hollywood. Except for his extreme hotness, he was down to earth, not full of himself or anything. What would it be like to have him as a boyfriend?

That would never happen. I was the kind of girl who guys liked, but never liked quite *enough*. They thought I looked good on the outside, but they lost interest once they realized I was a nice girl. And I don't mean the Dallas kind of nice — super hot and sexy. I mean the real kind of nice that didn't give it up for just anyone. And, idiot that I am, I fell for the wrong type of guy every time.

Stella would arrive soon, but until then, I wanted to hang out with Dallas — another wrong guy. Instead, I planted myself on Jackie's couch, flipped on the TV and tried to focus on something besides Jackie's life and her uber-hot ex.

The doorknob rattled and a moment later, Stella marched in. "TMZ filled their pages with you and Dallas. Could've been worse, I suppose. Everything went okay after you guys left the theater? Does he still think you're Jackie?" she asked as she hung her purse on the back of the chair.

I flipped the TV off and straightened my shoulders. "Yes, of course, he does."

"You sure?" She came into the living room for a closer look. "I've had a bad feeling since I woke up this morning."

I hated my life. No, I liked *my* life. It was Jackie's life I didn't want — except for Dallas. "I'm sure. But if something went wrong, Jackie couldn't blame you for it. Or me. I'm doing her a favor, because she begged."

"Geez." Her eyes narrowed as she dropped her purse on the sofa. "You're awfully defensive. Did something else happen last night?"

"No." Not *last night.* I avoided her gaze as I went to open the fridge. Not like I was hungry, but it gave me something to do.

Stella shadowed me to the kitchen and leaned

against the doorjamb. "Let's pretty you up and get this appearance over with."

I grabbed a soda, popped the top and slapped on a smile. "Yes, so I can hurry up and come back to this condo filled with Jackie's things." At least at home I had all my belongings — and my parents.

She sighed. "What's bothering you?"

I squeezed my eyes shut and pinched the bridge of my nose. "I hate lying to everyone, especially Dallas. It's hard."

"Because you like him." It wasn't a question. "And you know it won't go anywhere."

"Exactly," I said.

"Would it help if I came over tonight with a movie and popcorn? It might take your mind off him and keep you in the condo." She gave me a sympathetic smile.

"That definitely sounds better than brooding." I smiled. "Thanks."

"Good. We should start getting you ready if we're going to be there on time."

Stella dressed me in a mini skirt, a blouse that fell off one shoulder and, of course, a pair of heels specially designed to torture me. Lucky for Stella, it was daytime and she wouldn't be the center of attention, so she got to wear comfortable slacks with shoes that wouldn't require suicide watch.

~~~

The wide sidewalk in front of the restaurant left room for pedestrians while still allowing space for media and guests. Stella and I waited on the sidelines and smiled as cameras flashed and clicked. Cars honked as they passed, probably recognizing a few faces.

"You're doing great," Stella said, never breaking her smile. "Like I said, you're a natural."

"Feels phony," I said, trying not to blink as lights went off in my peripheral vision.

"You remember what to say if you get cornered with a microphone?"

"Yes, you drilled it into me when you were getting me ready. I'm happy to be here. Proud to support my good friend, Steve. Everyone should try the food. It's phenomenal."

"Great. Yeah." Stella's eyes narrowed. "But say it with some enthusiasm."

We took our places closer to the ribbon as Steve positioned the scissors to cut it. A series of flashes and clicks and the ribbon collapsed. Moments later, the crowd dispersed. Some guests went inside to sample the food — it was a restaurant, after all. I decided that was a good idea since I hadn't eaten anything since breakfast with Dallas.

Inside, it looked like a normal restaurant with tables strategically placed to maximize the number of seats while still allowing for safe passage through the large room.

What would've been used as the waiting area contained two tables, beautifully decorated with herbs, lilies and little blue flower clusters. And lots of finger foods.

Stella stuck close to me, which discouraged anyone

from interviewing me. "Check out all these cheeses and dips," she said.

"I just tried the basil and roasted bell pepper. It's divine on that bread." I flicked a thumb to my left.

Stella stepped away from me toward the dip or sauce or whatever they called it. Red hair appeared at my right. I instinctively shrunk back, but Lisa, the reporter from *Exposed*, closed in before Stella could return to her spot.

"Eating for two?" She smirked.

After the trash she wrote about me — or Jackie — I was in no mood to listen to her crap. The urge to leave right then rose up and I started to set my plate down to do just that. Wait, why was I giving Lisa any power over me?

"It doesn't matter what I say. You're going to make up your own story anyway," I fired back.

Her gaze faltered. Was that guilt I saw in her eyes? A moment later, she bounced back with a smirk. Guess not.

"Nice try," she said. "Picture this headline: Jackie Refuses to Deny Baby Rumors."

Stella squeezed between us and growled, "She's not pregnant, Lisa. Go find a *real* story."

Lisa's tone became syrupy sweet. "I guess the extra food is assuaging your grief over not landing that role, huh?"

Nudging Stella out of the way, I took a step toward Lisa as I looked her up and down. Stella cleared her throat and I stomped on the words at the tip of my tongue. Instead, I settled for, "No comment."

"Friends Worry Over Jackie's Erratic Behavior," Lisa said as though it were another dramatic news headline. She smirked.

A cold fury filled me. I couldn't believe how Jackie put up with this badgering. No wonder she'd been ready to crack. More of Lisa's lies were the last thing Jackie needed right now.

How did Lisa get away with being such a liar? Weren't journalists supposed to report the truth? People who attacked other people, just for fun, deserved what they got. I opened my mouth, ready to let Lisa have it, but Stella thrust an arm in front of me.

"Okay, you two," Stella said. "Lisa, why don't you go harass someone else? Far away."

She gave Stella a tight smile. "No."

"Good afternoon, ladies."

My head whipped around to see Luke Holtz, star of *Otherworld*. He wore a sexy grin and a white button shirt that fell over faded blue jeans. Just as gorgeous as he always looked on the show. "Lisa, nice to see you again," he said.

Her smile softened and her eyes gleamed. "Luke, what a surprise," she purred.

"I need to chat with Jackie for a minute. Why don't I come find you in a bit and we can catch up?"

"I'll be waiting." Lisa gave him a sultry smile. Her gaze rested on me a moment and her smile froze. Her eyes flicked over to her left, behind Luke and Stella. A man aimed a video camera our way, the little red light announcing it was doing its job. No doubt, the camera man got every minute of our heated conversation. After one last sneer, Lisa wandered off.

I blinked. "Uh...thanks for the distraction," I told Luke. Behind him, the cameraman followed Lisa.

"I've seen Lisa go after stories pretty hard, but I've never seen her be so bitchy. Probably because she knows she'll never be as beautiful as you," he said, his eyes gazing into mine. "No matter how skilled her plastic surgeon is."

Stella cleared her throat. "I wasn't told you'd be here, Luke. Trying to steal Jackie's thunder?" she said in a teasing voice.

"I make my own thunder. Which is anywhere my publicist sends me," Luke answered, his unwavering gaze resting on me.

Uh-oh. I knew that flirty look. Mr. I'm-hot-and-you-think-so-too was going in for the kill. But I wasn't playing. Even if I did have an itch to date one of my favorite stars, I'd choose Dallas and his dreamy gray eyes over Luke's too-suave green ones any day.

Both guys were blazing hot and both could eventually get any girl right where he wanted her. Luke would do it by flirting, and unspoken promises with his smoldering eyes, and sexy smile. Dallas would earn it the old fashion way by draping his jacket over a girl's shoulders when she's cold, or taking too-high shoes off her aching feet, or feeding her when she's starving.

As tempting as it was to ride Mr. I'm-so-hot's thunder, I'd always been an old fashioned girl. But all of that was a moot point, since both guys thought I was Jackie. I refused to flirt with a guy who didn't even know my real name.

"Well, thanks for getting rid of Lisa," I said, breaking eye contact with him for just a moment to finger a piece of cheese.

"No worries." He shrugged, then sent a meaningful glance to Stella. Hinting for her to leave us alone?

Stella wasn't playing either. "Jackie, we really should get going."

He swiveled until he had his back to Stella. "You said you were a big fan of the show. Thought you might like a guest spot. I can talk to the producers. If nothing else, you should visit the set."

Oh, that did sound exciting. But Luke's eyes hinted at strings attached. He seemed more like Jackie's type anyway. Which was exactly why I didn't want to blow him off. If I didn't burn that bridge, when my sister returned, she could date him if she wanted.

"Sounds great." I flashed him the same smile I'd given to the photographers moments ago. "I'll check my calendar and get back to you."

He leaned in and his lips brushed my cheek. "I'll see you soon," he whispered before vanishing.

I shivered.

"Oh, look. Your other date just arrived." Stella's tone held a world of disappointment. I didn't need to ask who she meant.

I scanned the restaurant. "Where?"

"Three o'clock."

Dallas was heading our way in jeans and black boots, with a faded black t-shirt exposing his muscular arms. Interviewers were already moving toward him. Others turned and snapped pictures. Moments later, he stood next to me.

"Upstaging or stalking me?" I beamed. When he was around, I didn't feel so out of place.

He laughed. "Stalking you would've been more fun, but no. Just thought I'd stop by and say hi to Steve. I texted you about driving together, but you never answered."

"Oh. I didn't see it come in." Which was the truth, since Jackie's phone was with Jackie.

"And it would be impossible to upstage Jackie Bloom. No one outshines you." He grinned, but immediately narrowed his eyes. "Apparently, Luke Holtz agrees."

So he'd seen Luke kiss my cheek. "You've got nothing to worry about. I hear I'm carrying your child."

His dark hair fell over his forehead and his deep gray eyes sparkled as the corners hinted at something wicked. Not Luke Holtz kind of wicked who swept you off your feet before you realized what happened, but the Dallas kind of wicked that slowly seduced you until you were completely under his spell.

Was he remembering our last kiss? Or maybe that was just *me* who couldn't stop thinking about it. I was in way over my head.

"I'm going to give Steve my congratulations," Dallas

said. "Will you be here when I get back?"

"We're leaving," Stella answered.

"I'll see you at home then." The way he said *home* sounded so intimate. He gave my hand a quick squeeze and I watched him stroll toward a makeshift stage where Steve was about to speak.

Stella cleared her throat and I glanced her way. She gave me a *what the hell are you doing?* look and I realized how I'd been so obviously lost in his eyes. Whatever. She wasn't my mother or my boss.

"It's fine." I lowered my voice for her ears only. "I can do this."

She shook her head. "Even Jackie would be challenged if she became the filling in a Luke and Dallas sandwich. Be careful."

~~~

Stella had a family emergency and had to cancel our plans to watch a movie together. She dropped me off at my apartment, promising to pick me up the next morning for the *Vanity Fair* spread.

I was alone again in Jackie's condo. After five minutes, I found myself roaming her house aimlessly and tapping my thigh.

Grabbing my cell, I dialed my sister. She needed an update.

"So you're doing okay?" I asked.

"A bit better. But hold on. Back up to what you said about Luke. He was hitting on me?"

"Yep."

"Intriguing."

I could almost hear her smile through the phone. "And he's definitely not married. At least there's that."

"Yeah," she sighed. "Luke-freakin'-Holtz. Damn. Too bad I didn't meet him two months ago. Right now, I can't imagine dating anyone ever again. I'm going to become a nun."

I laughed and we chatted about the last episode of *Otherworld*. After a few more minutes, we hung up, and I was idle again.

Taking pictures always relaxed me. It was therapeutic and might take my mind of my temporary neighbor.

I grabbed my camera and shot out the door.

~~~

I stayed in the Tesla to take pictures so no one would see me. I'd found a great spot in the hills to get a perfect shot of the Hollywood sign, then I cruised the Boulevard and snapped the Mann's Chinese theater and the Capital Records building.

Hunger eventually drove me back to the condo. Just as I exited Jackie's car, my phone beeped.

E/thing ok? Stella texted. Need a/thing?

I texted back that everything was fine and I'd see her in the morning, then I headed upstairs.

Dallas stood in front of his open door, staring down at a stack of papers in his hands. As I got closer, I realized they were photographs. In my sneakers, I could do what they were meant for — sneak. I paused right behind him and peeked around his shoulder.

"Bad lighting," I said.

Dallas jumped. "Didn't know you were there."

I grinned. "I know."

He returned my smile. "I just got my new publicity photos. I'm not sure I like them. What do you think?"

"Weird shadows around your eyes." My index finger waved over his face in the picture. "The background washes you out. And who picked out that shirt?"

"Sounds like you could do better." He raised one brow.

"Maybe. Depends if there's a good spot to shoot you." I went around him and let myself into his place. The days were long in the summer, so it was still light outside. I could probably get some decent pictures if he had a space with plenty of natural light. The living room had canned lighting, but I wasn't sure if they were bright enough.

He trailed after me. "You're serious?"

"Can't do any worse than those pictures, right?" I continued through his condo, scanning the spaces as I went.

He chuckled. "I guess not."

I passed through the dining room, making a mental note to return if I didn't find something better, then stopped in front of a door, unsure whether to barge in.

"Go ahead," he said.

I turned the knob and it opened. Light pushed

through white curtains billowing over a breeze from the open window. A very high king size bed was strewn with white sheets and a cream comforter.

Lots of white. Dark furniture. Perfect.

I walked to his closet and pulled out a white button down shirt, then tossed it at him. "Put that on. Do you have a pair of white pants?"

He blinked. "You know what you're doing?"

I lifted a shoulder. "You have another option?"

"Not anymore." He grinned and peeled off his t-shirt.

I turned around to avoid the sight of his touchable bare chest, and headed back to his closet. I really didn't need that six-pack to distract me.

T-shirts and jeans sat neatly folded on shelves. I sifted through the pants section until I found what I wanted. The off-white pair looked like something he'd wear at the beach. I plucked them off the hanger and exited the closet to find Dallas looking scrumptious in the white shirt.

"Your coloring looks good against white." I threw the pants at him and he caught them. "Put those on. I'll be back."

Inside my condo, I closed the door and leaned against it. Damn, he looked hot. I itched to bring out all that sexy and get him some fantastic shots. But I had to keep my mind on business. I'd have to and that was all there was to it.

After a few deep breaths, I headed back into his apartment. The clothes were perfect on him. I turned on my camera and checked the settings. "I want you on the bed," I said. Realizing how that sounded, I pressed my lips together.

"I was hoping you'd say that." A smile teased his lips.

"Wait." The bed hadn't been made and the sheets were rumpled — only on one side. I liked it. "Lie on that end by the window."

He obeyed, letting the mattress take his weight, then he leaned against the massive headboard.

I backed up and aimed. "Right arm up on the pillow above your head."

Click. Click. "That's great." *Click. Click. Click.* "Turn your head toward the window." *Click. Click. Click. Click.* "That's it."

"Give me a broody look," I ordered. He did the exact opposite, grinning. Perfect. *Click. Click.*

Doing this for a living would never feel like work. Maybe I'd reconsider my college plans...

"Show me what you felt like when you landed the lead in *Angel from Hell*," I said, as my finger tapped the button. "Now think about the last time you kissed a girl."

Oops. That last girl was probably me. It had better have been me. A slow smile crept up on his face as he turned toward the camera. Holy hotness. *Click. Click. Click. Click.* I'd definitely keep the pictures for myself. "Nice." *Click. Click. Click.* "Undo a couple of the buttons on your shirt."

He laughed. "I swear if you're trying to seduce me, I'm already there."

I forced myself to keep a straight face and not encourage him. Oh, Lord, but it was hard. I was in big trouble, because when he looked at me that way, my heart rate picked up as I imagined him laying a *real* kiss on me. "You want the pictures to turn out or not?"

"Can't I have both?" he answered, his fingers reaching for the top buttons.

"Shh!" *Click. Click. Click.* I set the camera on the foot of the bed, rearranged his legs and backed up again. *Click. Click.*

"I didn't know you were such a pro with a camera. Where did you learn?"

"My dad used to be a photographer for the army. When he opened the jewelry store for my mom, he realized he had a head for business and he liked managing. He still does publicity photos and that kind of thing on the side sometimes and I help him." *Click. Click.* "I did all the shots for our last catalog."

"Really? So you take time off from work to visit family and end up working?" Dallas asked.

Crap. Right. Today, I wasn't Maddie. I was Jackie. *Jackie.* "My dad was in a jam, so I helped out. Now stop talking and strike a pose." I grinned, hoping that would keep him quiet. "Okay, stand by the window." I waited while he did as I asked. *Click. Click. Click.* "Right hand on the window sill." *Click. Click.* "Don't look at me." *Click. Click. Click.* "Ooh, that's sexy."

He laughed and dropped his hand. I rested the camera on the bed again and closed the distance between us to roll up his sleeves a few inches. I paused a moment, then reached for the buttons of his shirt and set his gorgeous six-pack free. He looked much more relaxed, which fit the scene better. If the shirt caught a breeze, it would be a great shot.

"Perfect." My knuckles brushed his warm skin and I froze as the urge to kiss him nearly overpowered me. I raised my gaze to meet his.

Mistake. Big mistake.

"That's what I'm thinking," he said in a husky voice. His gray eyes darkened and he reached a hand up around the nape of my neck. He gently brought me closer and fastened his mouth to mine. Our tongues tangled, heat scorching my senses and dulling all the reasons why I shouldn't take more.

My hand raced up his torso and I pushed myself against him. He bumped against the window frame. Startled, he released me and stared, like he was trying to figure me out—which wouldn't have been necessary if I were behaving like Jackie would.

But I wasn't her. Maybe I kissed different than Jackie and that's why he looked confused.

I nudged him away and turned. "I'm sorry, but I can't do this."

His hands dropped. "You could a second ago," Dallas said, tilting his head. "What's wrong?"

More than anything, I wanted to tell him who I really was. That I wasn't Jackie and he'd only just met me. "It's just…"

"Is it Pete?" he asked softly. "Is it too soon?"

I burned to lay it all out for Dallas and tell him I didn't even know what Pete looked like. But how would he react when he found out I'd been lying to him? Even if he didn't care about the lie, I couldn't divulge Jackie's secrets to him. This was Jackie's life, not mine.

"You know..." He leaned on the window sill. "I watched my dad cheat on my mom for years. Doesn't matter how much that type of guy thinks he loves his wife—people like that care about themselves more or they wouldn't cross that line. Guys like Pete are only thinking of their own gratification, what *they* want. He could never have loved you the way you deserve."

I'd never looked at it that way. Of course, I'd never needed to since I wasn't the one who'd unknowingly dated a married guy. Regardless, Dallas's insight moved me. But just because he was a guy I could totally fall for didn't mean he would fall for me.

"Thanks." I stared out the window for a moment as I talked myself out of spilling my guts to Dallas. "Let's get a couple more shots and call it a day. Lean your shoulder on the other side of the window frame and put your left hand on the other side. Good. Face the window, like you're daydreaming."

Click. Click. Click. "Now turn only enough to look at me." *Click. Click.* "Okay, let's pack it up." I turned off my camera and slung its strap over my shoulder. "I can have these developed after my Vanity Fair shoot tomorrow. I'll come by as soon as I have them."

"So what's your fee?" His mouth curled up.

I laughed. "Let's see if they're any good first. If nothing else, it might give you an idea of what to go for next time."

"We're still on for tomorrow night?"

I bit my lip and dropped my gaze. After he'd just laid that delicious kiss on me, not a good idea to hang out with him. "We shouldn't..."

"If I keep my hands to myself?" he asked.

With those ground rules, it would work. Plus, it'd be fun to see Josh Adams. "We're on."

~~~

The photo shoot the next morning went smoother than I'd expected. Understanding the other side of the lens helped. The photographer, even though he asked for impossible positions too often, made me feel relaxed. He'd get excited if I gave him a pose he felt worked and that positive energy was contagious.

When he wanted a sultry look, I'd remember Dallas's kiss the night before. When he wanted passion, I'd think of Dallas's kiss the night before. The photographer got anything he wanted, with Dallas's image in my head.

At last, the photographer released me and I wandered the huge, high-ceilinged room, looking for Stella. I found her close to the exit on her cell phone.

Stella held up an index finger. "I'll call you back in a few minutes, okay?" She pressed a button on her cell and dropped it in her purse. "My brother got in an accident yesterday. That's why I canceled our movie."

"Is he going to be okay?" I asked.

"Yes, but he needs surgery. In a few minutes, actually. It's nothing serious, but I still need to be there for him. I didn't know what else to do so I called Dallas to come get you. Could've called a cab, but I wanted you with someone you knew and he's the only one I could think of who you'd feel comfortable with."

"It's fine." I stroked the back of her arm. "You should go be with your brother."

"Dallas will be here soon, but you have time to get changed."

Stella said goodbye and I dashed to the dressing room to throw on my jeans and tank, then headed toward the front door to wait for Dallas. He was already standing near the back door.

I beamed. "Thanks for coming to get me."

"Purely selfish. I wanted to see those pictures." He grinned.

"We dropped them off on the way here. They're probably ready now."

~~~

I waited behind the tinted windows of Dallas's SUV, while he went inside to pick up the photos. A blond girl about my age stopped to gawk at him. He disappeared into the photo lab and she whipped out her cell. Moments later, a brunette girl joined her. They stood near the entrance pointing and whispering.

Dallas came out and the girls called his name. He stopped and the blonde thrust a piece of paper and pen at him. As he scribbled on the paper, her lips moved. I rolled down the window of the SUV to hear them.

"So it is true you're back together with Jackie?" the blonde asked.

"Please tell us you're not back together with that skank," the brunette begged.

"You guys don't know Jackie at all. She's a great girl. You should meet her." He crooked his finger at me and they turned in my direction.

Fans were one thing, but these girls called Jackie, *me* in this case, a skank. I definitely didn't want to talk to them. No way.

He raised his brows expectantly. Damn. If I stayed in the car, I'd appear beyond rude. I grabbed the keys from the ignition and jumped out of the SUV.

I took the few steps to stand in front of the girls and held out my hand for the brunette with a smile. "Hi, I'm Jackie."

"Heather." She hesitantly shook my hand.

"I'm Katya." The blonde beamed and grabbed my outstretched hand.

I gave them my red carpet smile. "It's nice to meet you. Do you guys live around here or just visiting?" I asked them.

"We're visiting from North Dakota."

"Must be culture shock," Dallas said. He looked so

comfortable chatting it up with the girls, like talking to regular people was the most natural thing in the world. "Are you staying long?"

"For the summer," Heather answered.

"Can we get some pictures with you guys with us?" Katya asked, bouncing like she was about to leave her skin.

"Of course," he said.

"First, I want one of you two together." Heather whipped out her camera.

If you can't beat them, join them. I put my cheek next to his and smiled.

A few minutes later, on my way back to his SUV, I glanced over my shoulder to find both the girls aiming their cell phones at us. Video for youtube later, no doubt.

I climbed in and closed the door. "You were so nice to them."

"I'm getting déjà vu." He started the engine and studied me with squinty eyes. "Like you don't do this same thing every day. This is getting weird, Jackie. You thought they'd actually serve you alcohol at the premiere, you didn't know where the restaurant bathroom was after that, and lately you just look lost. It's as if we've never hung out. What's going on?"

Oops. "It's just been a long week."

"Are you feeling okay?" He reached a palm out to feel my forehead.

"I'm not sick or anything." I turned straight ahead, hoping he'd stop with the questions.

"Hey." He waited until I faced him again. "It'll get better."

Was he referring to Jackie's affair with Pete or the ridicule she'd received over that movie role? Or the pregnancy scandal I'd started? I shifted in my seat, hoping he'd drop the subject and wishing he'd get back on the road. A moment later, he signaled to merge with traffic. Whew.

I really needed to be more careful with what came out of my mouth, but I was getting so comfortable around him.

"Let's see the pictures," he said, glancing at the envelope in my lap. "C'mon. Open it."

I chuckled. "You can't give my photos your full attention and drive too. Just a few blocks and we're home."

Five minutes later, he waved to the security guard of our building, drove into the parking structure and stopped next to Jackie's Tesla. Stretching out an arm, he tried to snatch the envelope, but I held it up against the window, and quickly got out.

"No cheating." I darted into the elevator. Wrestling over the shots seemed fun in my head, but that wasn't the best way to stay out of trouble. I opened the envelope and pulled out the stack of pictures.

Dallas pushed the number of our floor, then peered over my shoulder. "Wow, that's not bad. Oh, I like that one." He snagged the stack out of my hands and held it low so I could see, too. "Much better than the ones I showed you yesterday."

He was right. The lighting was perfect and so was Dallas. I'd never seen him more gorgeous. And the one with the open shirt was right before he'd kissed me...

The elevator door opened and, as if I didn't exist, he shuffled to his front door, eyes fixed on the photos in his hand. "These are fantastic."

"Thanks." I grinned. "I asked the lab to put them all on a disc, so you could make copies any time you want. Disc should be in there."

His gaze met mine. "No, thank *you*."

"No problem." I checked my watch. "Still going out tonight?"

"Yeah. I'll pick you up at five?"

"See you then." I marched to my own door and went inside.

Oh, hell. Two hours until five o'clock. I liked Jackie's apartment. It was pretty and had a sweet view of the Hollywood hills. But it didn't make up for being alone, when all I wanted was to be with Dallas.

~~~

An hour and a half later, Dallas stood beside me in Jackie's enormous walk-in closet.

His gaze left Jackie's rows and rows of shoes for a moment to eye me appreciatively. "You look hot."

"Thanks." My cheeks flushed and I averted my gaze. "So what should I wear tonight?"

"That's why you lured me in here? I thought you wanted seven minutes in heaven." He gave me a lopsided grin.

I laughed. "Why would we need a closet when your kitchen or bedroom works just as well?"

"I agree," Dallas said, his fingers grazing my wrist.

I pulled away. "Dallas, maybe we should, you know, ease up."

His eyes narrowed. "You mean, like not go out tonight?"

"No." I shook my head. "I like hanging out with you, but maybe we should try harder to remember we're just friends."

"Sorry." He turned toward me, staring intently. "I was asking what was going on with you, but I'm beginning to wonder what's up with *me*. Last week I didn't have this itch to kiss you—and you wouldn't have let me if I had. It's weird."

"Like you said, it's been a rough week for me. Maybe it's rubbing off on you." I shrugged, knowing I needed to steer the conversation away from *us*. "So what should I wear?"

"Since when does Jackie Bloom ask advice on clothes? You know what you like."

"I want to know what *you* like."

"What I like?" His eyes smoldered as he took a step toward me, then paused.

I stepped back, but my mind flooded with fantasies of him. Damn. "You know what? I can pick out an outfit on my own."

He just stood there watching me, the corners of his eyes crinkling.

"Why are you here anyway? You weren't supposed to come over for another half hour." I carefully maneuvered around him until I'd reached the closet door. Once out, I released a breath.

Dallas shrugged, then grinned. "Bored."

"I'm so flattered." I suppressed a grin. "Hang on. I'll get dressed and we can leave early."

"Why do you have to change? You can't go wrong with jeans, especially those. You look spectacular." His gaze slowly skimmed up my legs and landed on my hips. "Like I said, hot."

Just *nice?* Dallas? What planet did Jackie live on? Because in my world, *nice* was not nearly enough to describe Dallas Bines. He was like a panther on the hunt, total predator, and he was all *man.*

"Great." I forced a smile, pushing away my fantasy of rolling around on the bed with him. "Then we can go any time." I needed to get him in public where he wouldn't be such a temptation.

~~~

"We've hung out a lot the last forty-eight hours. The other night at the premiere, breakfast the next morning, the restaurant opening, my photo shoot, your Vanity Fair shoot and now this." He leaned an elbow on the table. "We've crammed weeks of dating into two days."

I sat right next to him in a circular booth that faced

the stage. Twirling my straw in the ice water, I smiled. "These are supposed to be dates?"

"Nah." He waved a hand. "This kind of raw sexual energy is completely normal with buddies, right?"

Blunt. I had to love that about him. But... "What are we doing, Dallas? We already broke up once. Now, all of a sudden, you want to do a take-back?"

"If my memory serves, it was a mutual decision."

It was? I'd better not go there, since I had no idea what he and Jackie had talked about.

"But why now?" I asked.

He wagged his finger at me. "It's as if you're a totally different person."

I didn't want him to analyze the differences between Jackie and me. Actually, I kind of did. Why would he be interested in me and not my sister, the starlet? "Different person? How?" I asked.

"It's so easy with you now. Reminds me of what it was like with this girl I met one summer. We hung out almost every day talking about things my guy friends would never get into. Religion, politics, books — everything."

"You liked her," I said.

"Yeah, but she was just a friend. I think it'd be cool to have that kind of a relationship with a girl I really liked though." He laughed. "It sounds lame, right?"

He kept throwing me curves. "Not at all," I said. That kind of connection wasn't so hard for me to buy, not since I'd gotten to know Dallas. Who would actually expect a guy like Dallas, superstar who was adored by teen girls everywhere, to want that from a relationship? Most guys I knew around my age were only interested in getting laid.

"What does that girl have to do with me being different?"

"I'm getting there. Before you and I met, I'd seen *Love Rush.*"

I gasped. Though it was my favorite of Jackie's movies, I'd thought it was a little heavy on the romance for most guys. "Of your own free will?"

Dallas chuckled. "Only to make my mom happy. And I kind of fell a little bit in love with you. As an actor, I should've known better, but you were so convincing. And despite what you'd been through, it didn't make you bitter and you didn't lose your innocence."

Did he just say *in love*? "Dude, that wasn't me. It was the character."

"Like I said, I should've known better." He shook his head.

"So... what does that have to do with me being different than before?"

He scooted closer to me. "The first time I saw you in our building, I was a little star struck. I expected to feel that connection with you, but I never did, so I suggested we call it quits and you agreed."

"Yet here you are."

"Yeah, because now, I feel it every time I look at

you. It wasn't there and now it is. How do you explain that?" he asked.

Yes, how would I explain that, indeed?

Chapter Seven

And here we came full circle, back to the change in Jackie. "Well…" I stared at the white linen napkin on the table that was folded into a tiny mountain.

"Sometimes, things happen that make you see things with new eyes," Dallas said. "First, all that crap with Pete, then the Henley White fiasco. That's a lot to deal with."

I didn't want to talk about any of that, because I was bound to say something to demonstrate my lack of knowledge. My gaze remained focused on the table.

"Sorry. I shouldn't have brought it up," he said.

The lights dimmed and the music faded, saving me from a reply.

"I'd like to welcome you all this evening to Hank's Blues Club."

I peered past the guy at our neighboring table to the man on stage, tall and lanky with light, messy hair.

"Tonight, we have with us the beautiful and talented Tina Laws. Let's give her a warm welcome." Clapping erupted and, and after a moment, he continued. "And for one song, we have a very special guest, Josh Adams."

The crowd hooted and hollered. I clapped and grinned at Dallas, just as a light flashed at our side.

Paparazzi. I groaned.

"A lot of celebrities here tonight. Now I'm thinking my inside information was a little too convenient. Free publicity for Josh." Dallas cocked his head. "Why the long face? You're normally a huge supporter of that."

"Right." I grimaced.

He studied me a moment. "Two weeks ago, Jackie Bloom would've never complained about photographers."

I shrugged. "Temporary insanity. Next week, I should be back to my old self."

"I hope not." Dallas nudged me with his shoulder.

The server brought our pizzas and we lapsed into silence and ate. Tina Laws and her band did a soulful tune, then kicked it up with some guitar and the bass hummed at my feet. They followed that up with a bluesy tune and I shared a grin with Dallas.

My phone vibrated and I rummaged through my purse to check the caller ID. Stella texted, *E/thing ok?* I answered her with, *Eating w/ Dallas. Home soon. How's ur bro?* She answered right away. *Again?! Does Jackie know? Bro doing gr8. C u tmrrw.*

"I'm curious." He laid his fork on the table. "Luke was all over you yesterday at the grand opening. I expected you to cancel on me and go out with him."

"Oh." When I realized he was waiting for a more substantial reply, I dabbed my mouth with a napkin to stall. "He's not exactly gross."

He chuckled. "And?"

"Guess I've been watching my parents too long. Married almost twenty years and they still *like* each other. The Luke type would be fun for a little while, but when all that newness wears off, would I still *like* him?" I shook my head. "Probably not."

My stomach twisted. This time, my answer was so not something Jackie would say. I took another bite of my pizza and chewed. Dallas hadn't moved yet and the look on his face made my hands sweat. I had to think of something quick.

"After the whole Pete thing, I'm reevaluating my system for choosing the guys I date."

"I like this new Jackie." His mouth curved up and he leaned away from the table to watch the band.

"Me too." I threw him a smile and mimicked his movements, careful to keep a friendly distance from him. "I'm glad you brought me here."

He patted the spot next to him. "C'mere."

That spot would put me right up against him. "Friends don't snuggle," I reminded him.

"Of course, they do. All the time." He gave me a mischievous grin. "Hands to myself. Promise."

Just like every other time we'd hung out, this was a bad idea. Against my better judgment, I faced the stage and leaned into him, then he wrapped his arms around my waist. Warm tingles shot through my limbs.

I craned my neck to say, "I thought you were going to keep your hands to yourself."

"Trust me, there are other places my hands would rather be. You're getting off easy." He grinned.

Suddenly, I couldn't stop thinking of all the places his hands could go.

Josh Adams came on stage and did his one promised song. When it ended, I clapped until the applause died down.

"Should we hang out longer or get out of here?" Dallas asked, his breath tickling my ear.

And give up this heavenly snuggling? It was for the best. Damn. "We can go now, if you want."

He jerked his head toward the exit and rose before offering a hand to help me out of the booth. He didn't leave me much room, so I stood there sandwiched between the seat and Dallas.

"You're going to drive me crazy, aren't you?" he asked.

Me drive *him* crazy? Dallas had it totally backward.

"Oh, look who's here. Dallas, my boy, get up here," a voice sounded from the speakers.

Dallas and I looked to the stage where Josh was motioning toward himself and grinning. "Dallas is going to jam with us. Right, buddy?"

"You sing?" I asked.

"That's a matter of opinion," Dallas replied with a wry smile. "And taste."

"Well, get up there, so I can have an opinion, too." I shoved him toward the band, because I knew I'd probably never have another chance to hear Dallas sing.

He stumbled and glanced back at me. Oh, crap. Had Jackie already heard him sing? He flashed me a grin. I breathed a sigh of relief and returned to our table.

As he neared Josh, one of the band members thrust a guitar at him. Dallas pulled the strap over a shoulder and leaned into the microphone.

"I'm Dallas Bines. How's everybody doing tonight?" he asked.

Pandemonium ensued as the crowd—all girls from what I could tell—screamed at the top of their lungs. I joined in, slapping my palms against the tabletop.

"I'm not sure if I should thank Josh for coercing me into this." Dallas grinned at Josh, then faced the audience again. "Tina was great, wasn't she?" Dallas paused while the crowd cheered for the band—although not as enthusiastically as they had for him. "This is a song I wrote this morning. It's miraculous what inspiration you can get from kissing an amazing girl."

His eyes found me and I slouched in the booth. Maybe the photographers wouldn't notice I was the girl he was talking about. Cameras flashed in my direction and my hopes plummeted.

Not only did this sweet and totally hot guy just announce to the world that he'd written a song inspired by me, but he'd told everyone we'd kissed—including whoever was taking pictures. No doubt, those pictures would be slapped up all over the internet by the time we got home. Someone might have even caught it on video.

Jackie was going to kill me.

The purpose of not getting involved with him was to avoid the gossip magazines and so Jackie wouldn't be upset. Done and done. But I couldn't take back our previous kisses or his words a moment ago...which led me to wonder again what the point was in not kissing him again.

Dallas hummed a slow, throaty and incredibly sexy melody.

I didn't expect it, I had no clue

That the girl I needed would want me too

A stolen kiss she gave for free

Then I knew she was the key.

Dallas looked so rock-star sexy up on that stage. And his hot factor increased by a hundred knowing he wrote that song for *me*. My girl friends at home would be so jealous if they knew it was me he sang for and not Jackie.

He flashed me another smile and, oh God, I *so* wanted to make out with him.

My eyes fixed on him as he strummed the guitar and rasped the chorus into the microphone.

This world can be such an ugly place

Full of violence, hate and disgrace

But you smile and make everything right

I can do anything with you by my side

If it doesn't work out, we would've tried

No matter what happens, we still have tonight...

Oh, yes. We sure did.

Girls shouted over the roar of the stomping and clapping.

"Thanks for listening," he told the crowd, then handed over the guitar and made his way back to our table.

I rose again and we headed to the exit. "You wrote that for me?" I asked once we were outside.

"I only write songs for blondes." He flashed me a grin.

My cheeks heated up and I was thankful he was walking and looking straight ahead, not at me. "How did Josh know you sang?"

"He and his band played in my last movie. We jammed a few times during filming. Just messing around."

Dallas stopped at his SUV and opened the passenger door for me.

I climbed in, buckled my seatbelt and turned to face him as he got behind the wheel. "You deserve a record deal."

"It's just for fun." Dallas glanced over his shoulder to back out of the parking space.

Fifteen minutes later, we were stepping out of the elevator and onto our floor. We both paused in front of our respective doors.

"Coffee?" Dallas asked.

Jackie was already going to be pissed at me in the morning. But the damage was done.

I bit my lip, wanting to tell him I wasn't Jackie, but knowing I needed to say goodnight. Except that who knew when I'd get to hang out with him again? "Sure. My place."

I spun and went into Jackie's condo, leaving the door ajar. Once I was standing in the kitchen, I realized that all the times I'd made tea, I'd never seen any coffee, let alone the coffee maker. And did Jackie even take creamer in her coffee anymore?

Crap. Crap. Crap. I whirled around to face Dallas. "Uh...I just remembered I'm out of coffee."

"That's okay. I'm not interested in coffee." He closed the distance to stand inches away from me. "So why did you *really* invite me in?"

"Uh...you wanted coffee."

"Which you are lacking." He reached up to brush my hair off my shoulder, then his gaze moved to my exposed neck. He was looking at me the same way he had after breakfast, just before he'd kissed me.

"We could go to *your* place," I said. It would distract him from what I suspected he was about to do. Plus, if I got the feeling anything was about to happen between us in his condo, it would be easier to escape than getting him out of Jackie's condo.

Except I wanted to be trapped with him. No escape. Nowhere to run.

He dropped his arms. I expected him to back up and lead the way toward coffee across the hall. Instead, his hands clamped onto my hips and he turned me until I was flat against the kitchen cabinet. "You really want coffee right now?" he asked.

It was a perfect opportunity to kill the moment. All I had to do was say yes.

I let out a shaky breath, then tilted my face to meet his. "I only drink coffee with blonds."

"Excellent," he whispered and leaned into me.

I closed my eyes as his lips moved against mine and I opened for him, heat searing my tongue and traveling to my brain like a lit fuse.

Holy Mother of God.

I ran my hands over his wide shoulders and over-lapped them behind his neck, pulling him closer. I must have moaned or something, because he gripped my waist a little harder and pulled my hips against his. Denim brushed denim as one of his knees wedged between my legs. He angled his face to take the kiss deeper.

For every second he touched me, my IQ plummet-ed. Soon, I'd be completely void of any sense at all. But as delicious as Dallas was, I couldn't sleep with him. No matter how much my body needed me to give in. I hadn't known him long enough. Besides, he thought I was someone else. It wasn't right.

Too bad I didn't know left from right anymore. And as much as I told myself how wrong it was, it didn't *feel* wrong at all.

Dallas's hands crept up my waist, his thumbs pressing into my skin just above my ribs. Heat rushed through my body and my adrenaline kicked up.

An image of Jackie flashed through my mind. It didn't matter how charming Dallas was or how much

I liked him, he was still my sister's ex. Explaining one kiss or two was easier than explaining a full-blown make-out session. And, if I were to be honest with myself, I liked him too much to stop. But how could I justify sleeping with him to Jackie?

I let my hands slide down to his chest. With my palms flat, I nudged him until he released my mouth. His glazed eyes were half closed, like he wasn't anywhere near finished with me. The feeling was mutual. The last thing I wanted to do was stop.

He gave me a lopsided grin and brought both hands up to cradle my face.

Okay, one more.

Dallas kissed my cheek on his way to my neck and I arched to give him better access. His hair slipped through my fingers as my other hand gripped his muscular arm.

"You're so beautiful, Jackie," he whispered into my temple.

Jackie.

Reality hit me like an anvil.

I was lying to him and anything building between us would end as soon as he discovered my deception.

My heart hurt at the thought of leaving him. And I didn't even care anymore about avoiding the media. When I pictured myself with Dallas by my side, getting hounded by paparazzi seemed way worth it — whether they thought I was Jackie or just me.

At the risk of being the world's biggest tease, I dropped my hands to his chest again. "We should probably get some sleep. I had a great time though. Thanks for taking me out." I pushed, then again a little harder, until he was through the front door and standing in the corridor. "Goodnight."

So he wouldn't think I was upset, I smiled. He blinked, cocking his head, just before I closed the door and locked it.

And the award for most horrible sister goes to...

Actually, I was similar to Pete, in a way, putting my own desires above someone else I claimed to love.

Jumping onto the sofa, I covered my face as shame ravaged me. How could I ever look Jackie in the eye again?

Tomorrow, I'd end it with Dallas.

Wait. Who knew if I'd even see Dallas tomorrow? It's not like he'd asked me if I had plans. Maybe he had other things lined up. Then I'd end up agonizing over it until I ran into him again.

But he was awake *now*.

I darted into the hallway and knocked on his door. He opened it straight away, a slow smile spreading over his face at the sight of me.

I backed away and shook my head. "I'm sorry. I really am. But I can't do this."

"Jackie, what's wrong?"

"I can't see you like that anymore. This has to end. Now."

"Fine. We'll take it slower, like you said earlier."

"No." I shook my head. "I mean, I can't go there with you. Ever."

His brows lowered. "Because of Pete?"

Not directly. As I struggled for an appropriate answer, my gaze drifted to the cream colored walls of the corridor.

Taking my silence as confirmation, his face fell. "I don't get it. We have a connection. You feel it too."

Dallas was right, but we were over before we'd really even begun. To my horror, my chin quivered. "I'm so sorry."

"If that's the way you want it…" He looked wounded.

"Yes." I dashed inside Jackie's condo and slammed the door.

I'd known from the start that pretending to be Jackie would be a bad idea. If only that knowledge would take away the pain in my chest.

~~~

"Maddie!"

The earth moved around me and I braved the bright sun against my bleary eyes.

"Maddie, what the hell?"

My blurred vision focused. Jackie was sitting on the bed at my hip, waving several sheets of paper.

"Can you explain how you were out on a date, looking all cozy with Dallas, after our last conversation? While you're at it, tell me why he'd write a freakin' *song* for you."

Jackie thrust the papers at me. I didn't need to look at them. I knew what was there — photos of Dallas and me.

"Please tell me you didn't sleep with him. It would be too weird, Maddie." She scowled, but it sure beat the anger I'd expected.

I propped myself up by my elbows. "I didn't. I promise."

"Why go out with him at all?" Jackie's voice caught and she looked defeated as she pressed a finger to each temple.

"It was uncomfortable here with no friends or family." I sighed. "He made it bearable. I didn't expect hanging out with him would lead to kissing. I really didn't."

"But you did kiss him, Maddie. Do you realize what this means? I'm going to have to clean up this mess. I can't keep seeing him. You didn't... you didn't tell him the truth about our switch, did you?"

"No!" I leaned forward off my elbows. "And don't worry, I ended it last night." Even if I could face Dallas again and even if I had Jackie's blessing to confess, it's not as if he'd want me after finding out I was a big fake.

She released her breath in a whoosh. "Thank God."

"Is that why you're back, to avert a Dallas disaster?"

"No." She tilted her head thoughtfully. "I realized that hiding isn't going to get me what I want."

"True, but you don't need to rush it," I said. "Maybe I shouldn't go just yet, in case you need anything.

"Stay, if you like. I always love having you around. But don't do it for me. I'm okay now," Jackie insisted.

"After just a couple days?" I shook my head. "I don't know, Jackie. You were pretty upset when you left."

"I'm not saying coming back is easy. You're right, I was really upset. And poor Mom and Dad spent a lot of time listening to me whine. But once I got through that, I was more objective."

"What did you figure out?" I asked.

"Hiding from my problems isn't making them go away. In fact, the longer I stay away, the more screwed I am. I need to get back in the game if I want that part in *Winter's Edge*."

"Are you sure you're up for that?" I took her hand in mine.

"It was good to get away and regroup. I feel stronger. Pete was a jerk who doesn't deserve me, but wherever I go, I can't change what happened." She lifted her chin. "I *will* own that role. I'm going to have to fight for it though and I can't do that from our parents' house."

Yep, Jackie Bloom was back.

~~~

Jackie didn't keep much food in her kitchen, but we managed to scrounge up a decent breakfast. After she repeatedly assured me that she was going to be fine, I gathered what few belongings I'd brought and we said our goodbyes.

"Hey, don't forget this." She thrust a car key into my palm. The Tesla key.

"You brought my Beetle back. I don't need this."

"I promised it to you. A deal's a deal."

I screwed up my face. "But you love that car. I can't take it."

She smiled and backed away when I tried to return the key. "But you love it *more*. And you deserve it after walking the red carpet. You really rocked it, sis. I looked amazing."

I rolled my eyes. "What am I going to do with a car like that in Hemet?" Hemet...I'd be there soon. And further away from Dallas and any chance of being with him. But whether I lived in Hollywood or Hemet, we had zero future. Still, the thought of getting in a car and leaving made my chest ache.

"Not my problem." She grinned. "Park it in the garage, if you want, and visit it every day. I don't care. It's yours now."

The car was a small consolation for losing Dallas. "Fine. I'll hold it for you. When you're ready to have it back, let me know."

"I'll just go buy something else." She closed the distance, flung her arms around me and squeezed.

In a matter of minutes, I'd be driving away from Dallas. My eyes watered and I sniffed.

She drew back and studied my face. "Are you okay? Second thoughts about leaving?"

Staying was a bad idea. Besides, if Jackie and I couldn't be seen together, I'd be stuck in her condo all day. I already knew what kind of trouble that would lead to. But no way would I burden Jackie with my Dallas crush. I didn't want her to feel guilty—she had enough to deal with.

I forced a laugh. "Oh, please. You know how I hate this city."

"Okay. Drive safely," Jackie ordered. "I love you."

"I love you, too."

During the elevator ride down to the underground parking, I sent Stella a goodbye text. Then I started up the Tesla and mentally said goodbye to Hollywood and Dallas.

~~~

My chest ached and my vision blurred as I drove back to Hemet.

Dallas was just a guy and there was no shortage of them around. Millions of guys all over the world, right?

But none of them were Dallas.

Stupid Dallas. Why couldn't he be more like Luke Holtz? I wouldn't have had a problem leaving Hollywood then. But no. Dallas had to be generous to his fans, an amazing family guy, an incredible singer and he just *had* to write a song for me. To make it worse, he was sexy as hell and a fantastic kisser.

Oh, yeah, Hemet was over populated with guys like that. Not.

I wanted to turn the car around, spill everything to him, and beg his forgiveness for lying about who I was. I couldn't though.

I needed to snap out of it. I'd only known him a few days. Not nearly long enough to fall in love. No way.

Still…that's exactly what it felt like.

I'd get over him—eventually. In the meantime, I was a long ways from not wanting Dallas.

Chapter Eight

I grabbed a fresh tissue and wiped my eyes. I'd been up in my room since I got home hours ago, wishing I were in Hollyweird and missing it. Missing Dallas.

And there had been sobbing involved. Lots of it.

Curling up against my pillow, I eyed my cell I'd thrown on the bed earlier. I wanted to call Dallas just to hear his voice, but I'd never even gotten his phone number. Jackie would have it. I couldn't ask her for the number of the guy who'd dated and dumped her though.

"Sweetheart?" my mom called through my bedroom door.

I sniffed and dabbed my eyes, so she wouldn't know I'd been crying. "Come in."

The door opened and she poked her head in. "You've been home for a while. Don't you need to eat?"

"I'm not hungry." I gave her a weak smile. "But, thanks."

She sat on the edge of the bed. "Do you want to talk

about it?"

"No." I wrinkled my nose. "Not really."

My mom folded her hands and stared into her lap. "Jackie came home and cried the entire first day."

"Yeah, she needed a break."

"And now you're doing the same thing. She told me what happened with her, but that doesn't explain what's going on with you."

"I want things I can't have." Being more specific than that could lead to Jackie finding out I'd seriously fallen for her ex. She'd feel guilty and I didn't want that for her.

"Did you... do you want to move there?" my mom asked.

Did I? I missed Stella. And pretending to be Jackie made me realize how much I've missed having my sister close by. But did I want to live in Tinseltown? Living there, but not being with Dallas would be too painful. "No."

"Okay." She remained silent for what seemed like minutes, then rose and kissed me on the forehead. "When you feel like talking about it, let me know. Lasagna's in the oven, but I need to make a quick run to the store before dinner. I'll be back in a few minutes."

"Thanks, Mom." That's what I loved about her — she never pushed and would wait patiently until we came to her in our own time.

After giving my hand a pat, she slipped from my room and closed the door. Moments later, I heard my mom's car drive out of the garage.

I'd known Dallas only a few days. What I felt couldn't be love. And it was a good thing too, because he'd never love me back. I was the girl who'd lied to him and pretended to be someone else. That kind of betrayal was a crappy start for any relationship. Even if he did forgive me, that didn't automatically mean he'd want to date me.

If the guy I'd lied to and left behind were Luke Holtz, I wouldn't have to wonder what he'd wanted. Luke wouldn't go for plain Maddie when he could have a star like Jackie. Dallas was different though. He hadn't been into Jackie the first round.

Which brought be back full circle. Had we stood a chance if he'd known who I really was? The thought killed me.

I squeezed my eyes shut, determined not to start bawling again.

A car engine idled in front of our house, then suddenly stopped. Not driven away, but shut off. It didn't sound like my dad's car though, or my mom's. Yet, it sounded familiar. Like my Beetle, which I'd left at Jackie's.

Since our only neighbors lived far enough away that I needed binoculars to see them, whoever just parked at our curb had come for me or my parents.

I sprang off the bed, looked out the window and saw my Volkswagen Beetle hugging the edge of our lawn. What was Jackie doing back? Something was wrong.

Dashing out of my room, I zoomed down the stairs, darted outside and tore across our lawn, practically skidding to a halt just a few feet from my car.

Not Jackie.

Dallas climbed out of the car and planted himself directly in front of me. He stared down at me, his lips thinned to a straight line, his gray eyes dark.

"Dallas, what are you doing here?" I blurted without even saying hello. "Is everything okay?" By the look on his face, everything was *not* okay. The coward part of me wanted to retract the question and run back inside.

The scowl lessened just a bit. "We need to talk."

"Uhm…How did you get the key?" He'd gotten it from Jackie, obviously. Did that mean he knew I wasn't her? And why drive my car, instead of his own? But the bigger question banging around in my brain was why he'd come.

"Jackie gave it to me. And your address."

So he knew the truth. "Did she tell you or did you figure it out?" I asked.

"Jackie enlightened me." Dallas's jaw tightened. "But I want to know why *you* didn't tell me?"

"I-I couldn't. It wasn't my secret to tell and I swore to Jackie." But I still felt sick to my stomach for betraying him. Avoiding his gaze, I folded my arms over my chest. "A promise is a promise."

"Really, Maddie?" he growled. "You were just going to let me go? The last few days meant nothing to you?" He fisted his hands at his sides.

My eyes narrowed. "Did it mean something to you?"

He exhaled. "Would I be here if it didn't?"

He'd come all the way out here for *me*? Not possible. "But…guys like you don't go for girls like me. The real me, I mean."

His brows rose. "And why's that?"

I hesitated, shifting my weight from one leg to the other. "Because I'm not like those other girls that you know. I get a little nervous in crowds, especially in the spotlight. And I'm not exciting like the Jackie you thought I was. I may be boring by Hollywood standards, but I like myself the way I am."

"Guess what?" He inched toward me. "So do I."

Dallas had to be experiencing a moment of insanity, because he couldn't possibly like me back. "Why are you *really* here?"

Dallas blinked, then his words slowed. "For you, Maddie. It's only been one day and I miss you already."

"Really?" I asked, still skeptical. It's not that I didn't think I deserved to be liked. But how could he trust me after I'd deceived him like that? "Even though I pretended to be someone else?"

"Out of loyalty to your sister. Family's important." His voice softened. "And if you hadn't switched places with Jackie, we wouldn't have met."

Relief washed over me, but my smile faded. "You're still my sister's ex. Isn't that…weird?"

Dallas gently grasped my shoulders. "I hardly count as an ex. Two dates, one kiss and it was over."

"According to the magazines, you guys dated for weeks." I scoffed. "How could you only kiss her once after dating all that time?"

"Weeks, huh?" He shook his head. "Did you read that in the same rag that said Jackie was pregnant? We go places together, just as friends. You know, it's convenient since we're neighbors."

"Whether it was one date or twenty, there are unwritten rules about that kind of thing." I couldn't cross that line again. Jackie hadn't made a stink about it before, but she might if it went further. And I couldn't blame her if she did.

He kept his grasp on my shoulders. "But if you and I being together doesn't bother Jackie, why should it bother you?"

"How do you know she doesn't care?" I asked.

"She gave me this address and shoved your car key at me." He released me, but inched closer. "She also told me that the way to your heart is through jasmine. In pots, not bouquets, otherwise they die." He stuffed his hands in his jeans pockets and shifted his weight. "She warned me to make sure you had time to read every day or you might get grumpy and that you'd rather curl up with a good book than watch a movie. Then she said 'Good luck, stud. If you break my sister's heart, I'll have to hurt you.'"

I wrinkled my nose, unable to picture my sister playing matchmaker, especially with Dallas. "She really said that?"

"Promise." Dallas made the cross symbol over his heart.

So much for her soap boxes on being young and free to make mistakes. That would be kind of hard to do with a guy like Dallas who'd be in it for the long haul. But I had her blessing to date him, which meant that nothing stood in the way. "I can't believe she told you about our identity fraud when *she* was the one who insisted on not telling anyone."

"Oh, uh…" He turned away from me.

"What?" I asked.

"I kind of ambushed her in the hallway, thinking she was you, and demanded to know what the hell was going on. I told her it couldn't have been one-sided and that…"

I swallowed, not quite believing the words coming out of his mouth. "And what?"

He lifted a shoulder. "That I'd fallen for her. You, I mean. It was weird though. I was standing there in front of her door spilling my guts, but I couldn't figure out why we suddenly had zero chemistry."

Fallen for me?

"And that was when she showed me a picture of you guys together and told me you were twins."

"Then you drove all the way out here just for *me*?" I had to be sure.

He freed his hands from his pockets and looked like he might reach out to me, but he let them fall to his sides. "Maddie…I think we can be good together."

My eyes misted and I bit my bottom lip. "You and me?"

"Yeah, why not?"

Why not indeed? I'd gone from fame to shame, but now where did I belong? I glanced up into those eyes and knew my place was with him. "Will you stay in town for a while?"

One side of his mouth curved up. "Well, seeing as it's kind of a long drive back..."

"Speaking of driving, why did you bring my car and not yours? If things hadn't worked out, what would you have done?"

He entwined his fingers with mine. "I believe in us, Maddie. But the way you left, I wasn't sure if you did too. What if you bolted when you saw my car? So I brought yours, knowing you'd assume Jackie was driving."

I couldn't wipe the smile off my face. Not that I wanted to. "Make me breakfast in the morning?"

"So long as you don't leave my sight until then." He grinned.

I laughed. Sure, I was crazy about him, but spending the night with him? "Oh, really?"

"We'll rent a bunch of movies and fill up on pop-corn. Maybe snuggle. If you're lucky."

"I'm feeling very lucky right now." I leaned in and wound my arms around his neck.

He pressed me closer, his arms wrapping all the way around me, and buried his face in my hair. "I have to be back the day after tomorrow for that guest spot on *Love and Loathing*," he said.

Oh, right. We lived a two hour drive from each other. "Dallas, if you're there and I'm here, how will this work?"

"We'll figure it out." He brushed his lips against my forehead. "Jackie's got an audition next month for that role in *Winter's Edge*. Henley is finishing up another project, which gives Jackie time to research the role. She wants to rough it on a ranch—milk cows, rope steer, shovel horse manure—so she can give the character more authenticity when she tries out for it."

"Rough it on a ranch?" Jackie's idea of roughing it was skipping the limo and driving the Tesla herself. "You're serious?"

"She said you don't start college until the fall. Why don't you stay in her condo while she's gone? We can drive back together in the morning."

Dallas Bines, my dream guy, had just made a two hour drive in a girly car to take me back to LA. Me, not Jackie. I grinned. "This was *her* idea?"

"Yeah, well, she also wants you to pretend to be her for a while longer." He snickered.

I laughed. "I knew there was a catch." I wouldn't complain though. Jackie's request made it very convenient for me to date Dallas without moving to LA. Yet.

He grinned. "You know, UCLA is a great college. And LA has some pretty good photography schools."

"I'll have to look into that." I stretched up on my tiptoes, melted against him and kissed my fantasy guy.

The End

More Titles by Veronica Blade

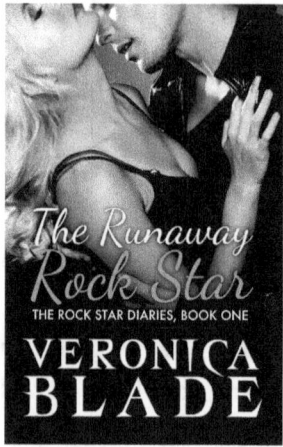

An infamous bad-boy rocker falls for a small-town girl who has no idea who he is. Considering his reputation, that's probably a good thing.

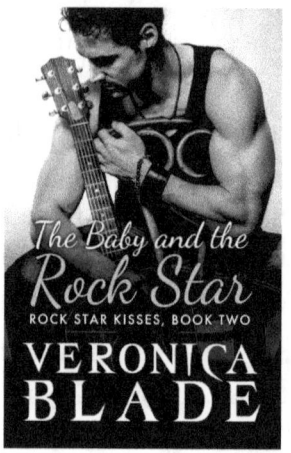

He's working hard to get his life back on track after three years of alcohol-induced oblivion. She can't forget their one wild night together—that he doesn't remember.

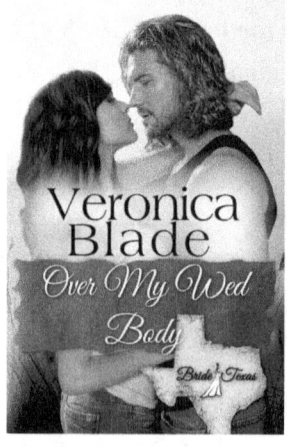

When Hunter realizes he botched the annulment of his marriage to his longtime friend, he must decide if she and their marriage are worth fighting for.

A micro trilogy including Single-Handed, Singled Out (book two) & Single-minded (book three).

More Titles by Veronica Blade

Should a woman who's unable to forget her first love give "happily ever after" one more try?

A Cinderella who spends her nights as a wolf. A prince with a taste for blood.

SHAPES OF AUTUMN SERIES

Thrown to the Wolves: The Legend of Hannah & Eli (prequel)

My Wolf's Bane (book one)

Wolves at the Door (book two)

Dead Wolf Walking (book three)

The Dark Wolf (book four)

Lord of the Wolves (book five)

Different species. Mortal enemies. It'll never work, but they'll die trying.

A newbie witch enlists help from the scrumptious school bad-boy to make her life and death choice between two battling covens.

The witch queen must make the impossible choice between abandoning the throne and her people, or spending eternity without the man she loves.

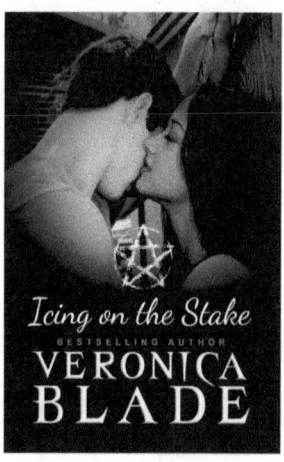

Sofia lays her hard-won anonymity on the line by saving the most popular boy in school. Worse, she's been exposed to the vampire hunters who attacked him.

)

For updates on releases,

please visit VeronicaBlade.com

Acknowledgements

I have so many people to be grateful for! Thank you to all my beta readers — Sara, Sausha, Danette and a few others. A very special thank you to author Susan Hatler for all her work on *From Fame to Shame* and her suggestions to make it even better. Susan, you rock!

Thanks to the team at Crush Publishing — editors Robin Haseltine and Sarah Billington and a very special thanks to Rose Nomura for her fabulous cover design!!

Free e-Book Offer

For a limited time, *Thrown To The Wolves: The Legend of Hannah & Eli (Shapes of Autumn Prequel)* is available for free from my website.

Find out more at VeronicaBlade.com

About Veronica Blade

Veronica Blade lives near Carson City, Nevada with her husband and furbabies but also spends a lot of time in southern California. She writes sweet romances to live vicariously through her characters. Except her heroes and heroines lead far more interesting lives—and they are always way hotter.

)

You can visit Veronica Blade on Facebook, check out her website at VeronicaBlade.com or follow her on Twitter @VeronicaBlade. You can even e-mail her at veronica@ veronicablade.com. She loves hearing from readers!